Real Love from a Boss

The Tale of Kon & Sapphire

Nechol

A dream written down with a date becomes a goal. A goal broken down into steps becomes a plan. A plan backed by action makes your dreams come true.

-Greg Reid

A word from Nechol:

I would like to thank God first, because without you nothing is possible. I also want to thank my kids, Jacori and Sa'Ryiah, because without you I would have no motivation to push as hard as I do. To my sister Kieasha, you will be forever missed! Thank you to everyone that purchased this book. You are in for an unpredictable, emotional journey. I hope you enjoy the ride. Happy reading

Make sure you check out KissedbyRyy on IG and Facebook and at www.Kissedbyryy.com

Synopsis

There are only so many accusations a man can take, and Kon has reached his limit. Attempting to make things work with the mother of his child isn't working any more, and after a lot of decision making, Kon calls it quits with his longtime girlfriend, Chrissy. As he journeys to find himself, Kon finds Sapphire, but it couldn't have been at a worst time. If things couldn't get more hectic, Kon finds himself in the middle of a massive turf war and the person behind it, he has more history with than anybody else. But when it comes to betrayal, will Kon turn a blind eye? Together, will Kon and Sapphire be able to make it through or will they lose everything they love, including their lives, in the process?

Sapphire Snow

"**W**hat the fuck are those!" My eyes expanded as I pointed at the white lilies as the florist brought them into the building. "I specifically asked for bellflowers. What the fuck are those!"

"I'm so sorry. We must have got the shipment mixed up," she quickly apologized.

"How the fuck can you mix up a got damn shipment? What the fuck am I supposed to do now! The wedding starts in thirty minutes!" Pinching the bridge of my nose, I tilted my head back and released a breath.

I had been planning this wedding for months now, and the last couple of days seemed like hell. Nothing was going as planned and I found myself having to fix shit. First, the baker told me they were going to be able to make the cake I asked for. When I went to see the test cake, it was nothing like I envisioned. I found myself having to find another baker at the last minute and having to pay extra for them to put a rush on the order.

The bride called me crying because instead of losing weight, she gained five pounds and couldn't get into her wedding dress. I don't know what the fuck she thought was going to happen when every time I saw her, she was eating fucking junk food. I'm surprised she hadn't gained more weight than that. Luckily for her, I had a seamstress on hand and that was an easy fix.

No matter all the hectic shit that had been thrown at me, I still loved the shit I did. The result is what made me keep pushing forward. To see the bright smiles on my client's faces was everything to me. And because I took such good care of them, they stayed recommending me to the next person, and business was never slow for me. *Phire Events* was one of the top-rated event companies in Miami and I intended on keeping it that way.

"I'm so sorry. Do you want me to go back to the shop and see if we have any left there?" Amber questioned me, bringing me from my thoughts.

"No. I'll just have to make do with what I have. Sasha!" I yelled, waiting for my assistant.

"Yes, Sapphire?" She appeared almost out of thin air.

"Take that shit and put a little sparkle to it or something."

"But those are—"

"If you say it, you're fucking fired."

Nodding, she grabbed the flowers and quickly disappeared. This was my first time using Amber for flowers and was going to be the last. That hoe was getting a negative ten review on yelp by the time the evening was over.

Time was winding down, so I popped into the room to check and make sure the bride was all right.

"You look amazing," I told Sherry, easing behind her as she stared at herself in the mirror. She wore this beautiful mermaid white sequin gown and her hair flowed down her back in spiral curls. A custom-made tiara sat on top of her head. I was blown away when she first showed it to me. The shit was made with real diamonds. Whoever her husband was, that nigga had to have been getting the bag. The entire wedding cost two-hundred and fifty thousand dollars and that wasn't including what they were paying me.

The entire time I planned their wedding, I had to yet lay eyes on her husband. Every time he was supposed to be present, she had some excuse about his job preventing him from being there. I didn't care if he showed up or not, long as he made sure to deposit my check.

"Thank you." Her lips curved up into a smile.

"It's almost that time. You have five minutes."

"I can't believe I'm getting married today." She turned and faced me.

"Believe it. You're about to walk down that aisle and marry the love of your life. It's a beautiful feeling."

Here I was, telling her some shit that I knew nothing about. I was single. I didn't know a damn thing about getting married except for what I've observed. I've never even come close to getting married to anyone. Most men wanted a woman they could control and thought that the woman was supposed to go to work, come home, cook, clean, and make sure the house was in order. I wasn't that woman. I guess that's why no one thought about marrying me.

"I just want to thank you for making my dreams come true." Tears pooled at the brim of her eyes.

"Don't you dare," I told her, fanning her eyes. While I was sure that she wouldn't ruin her makeup because of the finishing spray, I didn't want her wasting her tears on me. I did what she paid me to do—make her dreams come to life.

Sherry's arms quickly wrapped around me, and she pulled me in for a hug. Sniffling, she said, "Okay, let's get this over with." A smile passed her lips and she tread toward the door.

"It's showtime." I rubbed my hands together, smiling. I knew the moment she walked into her wedding the floodgates were going to open. It was one of the most beautiful weddings

I've done so far. Winter Wonderland was the theme I always wanted to do for myself and when it came to Sherry's wedding, I perfected that shit.

Pressing my headset, I spoke, "The bride is on the way."

Sasha met us halfway down the hallway with the bouquet. She worked her magic making the lilies come to life with sparkling diamonds.

"Everyone's already lined up and ready to make their way down the aisle," Sasha announced, slipping to my side. I nodded and pressed the headset again.

"Cue the music."

Kem's "Share My Life" began playing and the white curtains pulled back. The entire room was white and silver with a hint of blue. All the guests wore different shades of silver while the bride and groom wore white and the wedding party wore blue.

Fake white trees lined the aisle. A white carpet led to the alter. I watched as Sherry's eyes lit up as she admired the entire room.

"Go," I whispered, nudging her a little bit because it seemed as if she was glued to the floor.

Soon as her feet touched the carpet, the curtain closed behind her, and I rushed off to the side door to make sure everything was going accordingly. Easing the door open, I slipped in quietly just in time to see Sherry make it to the center of the aisle. My eyes went to her husband-to-be and my mouth dropped to the fucking floor. I moved a little bit further to make sure my eyes weren't playing tricks on me.

"Jonathan?" I called out his name to see if he was going to answer me or not. His eyes darted in my direction and my heart dropped to the pit of my stomach. His jaw muscles tightened, and he shook his head. I knew that probably meant he wanted me to shut the fuck up, but he must have forgotten who the fuck he was dealing with.

Sherry stopped in the center of the aisle and her eyes landed on me as I neared Jonathan. I couldn't believe this shit. She was about to get to married to the nigga that had been busting down my pussy for the last four months. We weren't in a relationship, but he damn sure made it his mission to get this pussy at least three times a week. I don't understand how the fuck he was doing that shit when he had a damn fiancée at home. That's one of the reasons why I didn't trust these niggas now. It seemed like forever since I'd been in a relationship. Glad I didn't give this motherfucker my all because I would have truly been upset to know he was getting married.

The only reason I was about to say something now was because I liked Sherry. She had grown on me over the last few months and I wouldn't want her to end up marrying this pig, thinking he was her dream guy, when he couldn't even keep his fucking dick in his got damn pants.

The music turned off and I was sure all eyes were on us.

"Do you mind telling me what the hell is going on?" Sherry asked from behind. Her voice grew closer, so I knew she was approaching us.

"Do you want to tell her or should I?" My head tilted as I gazed at Jonathan. He looked as if he wanted to knock my head clean off my fucking shoulders. That was the least of my fucking worries. I could handle myself and even if I couldn't, there were security guards out there that were more than capable of tossing him out on his ass, groom or not.

"Why you have to come in here and start shit? What the fuck are you doing here anyway?"

"If you had bothered to show up to any of the meetings, then you'd know I was the one that threw you guys this beautiful wedding."

If he had bothered to show up, I could have saved them a lot of embarrassment and a damn good bit of the money they spent on the occasion.

"Jonathan?" Sherry's voice cracked. I felt bad for her. To be in this position with all eyes on you, it had to be embarrassing as fuck.

"I don't know what she's talking about," he swiftly lied, and she turned her attention to me.

"Sapphire?" She stared at me with pleading eyes. I knew she desperately wanted to believe him, but I wasn't about to stand here and fucking lie to this woman's face. If she chose to stay with him after finding out the truth, then that was her business, but I wasn't about to deny her the truth either just to satisfy his ass.

"I've been sleeping with Jonathan for the last four months. I didn't know he was your fiancé. I didn't even know he was in a relationship."

"How do I know you're telling the truth?"

Taking a couple of steps towards her, I leaned my mouth near her ear and whispered, "He has a mole on the left side of his dick, and it curves to the right." Stepping back, I noticed the frown on her face. She couldn't deny the fact that I'd slept with her fiancé.

"You son of a bitch!" Charging towards him, she smacked him across the face with the flowers. "How could you do me like this!" I could hear the pain in her voice. The last thing I wanted was to hurt her.

"You see what the fuck you started!" Jonathan barked as she smacked him across the face again. The bouquet ripped to pieces. Flower petals dropped to the floor.

"I fucking trusted you!"

Smack!

"Look what the fuck you did," a masculine voice said as a specimen brushed past me. He grabbed Sherry, pulling her off Jonathan to separate them.

"The weddings off!" she shouted, tears streaking her face.

"You really gon' let this bitch come between us?" Jonathan quizzed her, but she gave him the hand.

"Who the fuck is you calling a bitch!" Fumes spewed from my ears. This nigga was mad at me because he got fucking caught. No one told him to climb between my fucking legs, knowing damn well he was about to get fucking married. If I had known he was engaged, I wouldn't have ever wasted my fucking time with him.

Stepping to me, he said, "I'm talking to you, bitch." And mushed me in the head.

I whacked his hand away. One thing I didn't fucking play about was people putting their fucking hands on me.

"I don't know who the fuck you think you're talking to, but nigga, you got the right one."

"I'on see how you got a business; you're unprofessional as fuck."

"I'm very professional. It's motherfuckers like you that I have to remind that I'm from the hood too, and I'll whoop your fucking ass if you keep got damn playing with me."

Sherry stormed back down the aisle with the guy directly behind her. I wasn't certain who he was supposed to be to her, but it seemed to me like, he didn't play any fucking games when it came to that one.

"Alright, let's pack up!" I twirled my index finger in the air, letting everyone all my employees know that it was time to clear the fucking building. Sherry made her decision to end the wedding, and now we had to clean up everything. Luckily for me, I already got my payment deposited into my bank account.

I sure as hell wouldn't see a fucking penny waiting for Jonathan to pay me after the stunt I just pulled.

The guests cleared out of the room and exited the building. As Sasha and everyone else on my team, cleared out all the décor, I found my way to the reception hall behind the bar and grabbed a bottle of Hennessey. I needed something to take the edge off before I went completely insane.

Before I got there this morning and began decorating, I never thought the day was going to end with me breaking up the wedding. This shit definitely goes down in the worst events ever journal. Damn right, I kept a journal of all my failed events, so I'd know what not to do at the next one. I'm glad as hell this wasn't a huge client or else my business would have suffered behind this shit—drastically.

Plopping down on the barstool, I popped the bottle open and turned it up.

"Is this really what they paid you all this cash for?" There it goes again... that masculine voice.

I took another swig from the bottle and he occupied the stool beside me. "Did I say I wanted company?"

Cutting my eyes to him, I noticed he was a damn good-looking chocolate brother. From what I could see, he was tall... maybe a good six-two. I loved myself a tall brother especially since I wasn't that short. Spinning on the stool, I gave him my undivided attention.

"Does it look like I give a fuck 'bout what you want?" He snatched the bottle away from me and turned it up.

Rude much?

I admired his jet-black waves that spiraled out of control on his head. It let me know that he cared about his appearance. It took time to get waves like that.

"You broke my little sister's heart. Normally, motherfuckers ended up with a toe tag after some shit like that," His eyes embraced my frame. "But for you, I'll make an exception."

The corner of my mouth curved into a smirk. "And why is that?"

I gazed at his plump lips and the golds peeping through them. He had a neatly trimmed beard with a little fuzz directly underneath his lower lip. His mustache was fine, just how I liked it. His face was chiseled to fucking perfection. Tattoos sprouted up his mocha neck and my pussy throbbed. Tattooed men weren't my thing, but I was definitely ready and willing to give the shit a try. This man was so got damn fine, that I wouldn't even mind if he wanted to take me right then and there. I was going to a hoe today.

Taking one final gulp, he placed the bottle on the bar and rose to his feet. "'Cause, I might need you one day." Was all he said, and he strolled off.

Konfidence "Kon" White

Sherry's wedding was destroyed beyond repair. I felt bad as fuck for my little sister when she rushed off crying because shorty decided she wanted to drop that fucking bomb on her. She could have done that shit behind closed doors. If she wasn't so got damn fine, I would have placed a got damn bullet in her ass for hurting my little sister.

There were a few things I didn't fucking play about: Sherry, my money, and my motherfucking time. Ever since Sherry was fifteen, I fucking raised her. Our parents died in a car crash leaving us behind. The system thought they were going to get their hands on her, but that was a motherfucking lie. I was eighteen at the time and took her underneath my wing. I may not have known shit about raising another human being, but I made do. She turned out all right in my eyes.

Sherry was the reason why I ended up in the game in the first place. I had to make quick money to make sure we both were able to eat and have a roof over our heads. We stayed in our parents' house until I decided it was time for me to fucking take over and snatched every got damn thing from this nigga Dank that I was working for. Nigga didn't even see the shit coming. I placed a bullet in his skull and been running shit in Miami ever since.

Miami was my motherfucking city. Didn't a damn thing move without my knowledge. I had every motherfucking thing on lock except for my own love life. That shit was dragging me the fuck down. My girl, Christina was driving me fucking insane. That motherfucker thought I was cheating on her every time I left the fucking house. I was dreading going home at the moment for that exact reason.

Hitting the fob on my black Maserati, I hopped in the car. Since the wedding was over, I was going to go home. She was already pissed the fuck off that she wasn't invited to the wedding. Sherry couldn't stand her fucking guts and didn't want her anywhere near her shit. This motherfucker thought I didn't want her to go because I wanted to take someone else. We had that very fucking argument before I left the house this morning.

My phone rang and I leaned back, pulling it from my pocket. Blessed's name flashed across the screen. Blessed was my best friend. That nigga was my day one ever since we were in diapers. I didn't even call him a friend, he was more like a fucking brother to me. That nigga always had my back and was the only person I trusted with my fucking life. Our bond was so fucking airtight, I wasn't worried about a needle piercing that shit. Placing the phone up to my ear, I pulled out of the parking lot.

"Yeah?"

"You might want to get to the warehouse."

"What's going on?"

"I caught something. Just get here."

The call ended and I dropped my phone into my lap. I knew nothing good could come from what I was about to walk into.

Whipping in and out of traffic, I tried my best to get to the warehouse as quickly as possible. Normally, Blessed would handle shit on his own and just tell me about it later. Something bad must have happened if he was hitting my line and trying to drag me into the shit.

Pulling in front of the back entrance to the warehouse, I leaned over and grabbed my strap out of the glove compartment and cocked it. I always kept a piece on me no matter where I went, but out of respect for Sherry, I left it in the car for her wedding. She had already let it be known that she didn't want any nonsense going on. It was supposed to be her big day and she wanted it to be peaceful, but she wasn't that lucky.

Climbing out of the car, I went into the building. Screams could be heard in the distance, so I followed them to see what the hell was going on. Stepping into the main lobby of the warehouse, I stopped, noting the blood on the floor in front of Blessed's feet.

"Ahhh!" someone screamed at the top of their lungs.

I slowly rounded Blessed to see what the fuck was going on. He had one of our lieutenants on his knees in front of him with blood dripping from his head and face.

"What the fuck is going on?" I quizzed, pulling my suit jacket off, draping it over one of the metal chairs.

"I caught our little friend here when I got here. He tried to lie and say he was looking for us."

"What would you be looking for us for, Derek?" I rolled the sleeves up on my shirt and asked. "Today isn't drop off, and I'm sure when you got here, you didn't see any other cars, so why the fuck was you here?"

Derek's body trembled as he gazed at me. He knew he fucked up and there was nothing he could do about it. Even though he had access to the warehouse, Blessed and I were the only ones that could get in the vault room with the weapons, cash, and the storage unit where we kept all the product.

"I ran out of product," he lied, and from his facial expression, I could tell he was lying to my got damn face. He'd say anything to save face.

"If you ran out of product, you should have called one of us. I don't think the shit was possible since all the traps just re-upped a couple of days ago. You've never been the type to get shit off that damn fast. You mind trying that shit again?"

Pulling my piece from my waistline, I held it in front of my crotch and gazed at him directly in the eyes waiting for his answer.

"I—"

"Wrong answer."

Pow!

I sent a bullet crashing through Derek's skull, and his body dropped to the floor. I didn't have time to waste, standing here, listening to the bullshit seeping from his lips. That nigga wasn't going to tell the truth and even if he did, he knew he was still going to fucking die anyway.

"Call the clean-up crew," I told Blessed, tucking my gun back into my waistline. I grabbed my jacket off the back of the chair. "I'm heading out."

"You 'bout to take your ass home to Chris, huh?" A smirk crept up on his face. Even Blessed knew the fucking problems I had with this girl.

"I can already hear her mouth." I shook my head.

"I keep telling you that you better get rid of that girl before she is your fucking downfall."

"She cool," I said, and treaded towards the exit.

Hopping back into my car, I headed home, dreading even going there. It wasn't late, so I knew that she wasn't going to be sleep unless she was out with her friends. Those hoes weren't shit either. All they did was sit around and fucking complain about the exact niggas they were cheating on and shit. Chris knew that if she even thought about opening her legs to another nigga, I was going to fucking wring her got damn neck.

I pulled up to my mini mansion that sat on the beach and parked directly in front of the door. Having a house on the beach wasn't all that ideal for me. Chris was the one that fell in love with the idea and I tried my best to fulfill her desires. That's just the type of nigga I was.

She and I had been together for the last nine years. Shit was sweet in the beginning, but at this point, I wasn't sure how shit was going to turn out for us.

Hopping from the car, I entered the house and punched in the security code to stop the system from beeping. Heels clicked against the marble floors, nearing me. Taking a deep breath, I prepared myself for the bullshit that I knew she was about to bring my way.

Climbing the steps, I was met by her beautiful face that wore a scowl. When I first met Chris, I thought she was the most beautiful girl in the fucking world to me. She had these long gorgeous legs, big pouty lips, and short platinum blonde hair. She wasn't the curviest woman in the world, but she had enough for me.

"You're home early. I was just about to go out with Serenity and the girls."

"What's stopping you?" I asked, treading straight past her for Stormie's bedroom. I wanted to check on my nine-year-old daughter before I went into the bedroom to take a shower. Stormie was my pride and joy. It was the best thing I could have gotten out of my relationship with Chrissy. When the bullshit started, sometimes she got me to thinking that I wished I never met her, but then I wouldn't have my daughter.

Peeping into the room, I noticed Stormie wasn't in her bed like I thought she would have been. "Are you serious right now!" She stormed behind me.

"Where's Storm?"

"At my mother's. Were you not listening to me when I said I was about to go out? I see that's the only thing you're worried about."

Without saying another word, I tread to my bedroom. I was ready to get out of these clothes and settle in my mancave for the remainder of the day.

"Can you not start this shit right now? I had a long fucking day and don't feel like hearing the bullshit."

"What happened to you being at the wedding? Did your little date cancel on you or something?"

"Do you not know how fucking stupid you sound right now?" I tugged my shirt out of my pants and unbuttoned it. If I did take a date and she had canceled on me, I'd still be there at the wedding. It was my sister's wedding. That was my priority— to be there for her. Some of the bullshit that flew from her lips, I just didn't fucking understand.

"So, I'm stupid now?" She stopped, tilting her head to the side.

"Did I fucking say that?" Here she was, twisting my got damn words again.

"That's what the fuck it sounds like to me! What bitch were you out with, Kon!"

"How many times do I have to tell you that you're the only bitch I'm fucking?"

Treading into the bathroom, I turned on the shower and felt something slam down into my back. When I turned around, Chris was swinging all out of control and shit. This motherfucker was going to make me fuck her little ass up.

Swiftly gripping her by the wrists, I gazed down into her eyes and said, "What the fuck I told you 'bout putting your got damn hands on me? I don't put my hands on you, so keep those shits to your damn self." and lightly shoved her back away from me. She mugged me with tears in her eyes. This was the very fucking reason why I didn't want to bring my ass home. She made me want to stay out all hours of the night whenever she got to fucking acting like that.

"I just want to know the truth." Tears streaked her face as she gazed back at me.

"I told you the fucking truth. You know where the fuck I been at. My sister canceled the wedding, so I brought my ass home. What the fuck 'bout that you can't fucking understand?"

Undoing my pants, I shoved them to the floor and her eyes zeroed in on my dick. Chris thought dick was supposed to help every fucking situation.

"I'm sorry, babe." Her frame crashed into mine and she stared up into my face. "I know that a lot of bitches be behind you and I get to thinking the worst."

"You need to chill with all that insecure ass bullshit." Pushing my boxers down, I climbed over into the tub and she just stood there, looking dumbfounded as fuck. If Chris kept on with the bullshit, she was going to drive me the fuck away.

"I'm going out with Serenity. I'll be back later," was all she said before leaving out of the bathroom.

I finished up my shower, tossed on a pair of boxer briefs and went downstairs to my mancave. My mancave was my sanctuary in this house. Whenever I needed to ease my mind, I found myself locked away in there for hours at a time, facing a blunt, playing my PlayStation or engrossed in some show. Hopefully, this blunt and a good game of NBA would take my mind off shit for a bit.

A couple of days later...

The Miami sun beamed down on me as I sat on the steps of Everly Elementary school. I had been sitting out there for fifteen minutes, waiting for one of my student's parents to show up and pick them up. They were supposed to have been there, and I was growing impatient as fuck. I already had spent all day with my children—I'm not saying they were bad or anything, but I was tired as hell and wanted to go home and kick off these fucking pumps that were damn near strangling my feet.

"Do you want me to try and call someone else and see if they can come to pick you up?" I asked Stormie as she fiddled with her fingers.

"He said he was coming," she answered, not bothering to look up at me.

Sighing, I stared out at the almost empty parking lot. Most of the teachers and staff had already headed home. If it wasn't against the policy, I would have taken her home myself, but I wouldn't even know if someone was going to be there when we arrived.

I'd been teaching for the last five years. Ever since I was young, I always wanted to be a teacher. I loved the way they were able to help their students' progress and that's all I've ever wanted to do. I remembered when I used to line my dolls and bears up in my bedroom and pretend as if they were my students. The moment I walked across that stage and gained my degree, I was excited as hell.

Everly was the first school to give me a chance and so far, I loved it. It was days like these that pissed me the fuck off. If you knew that you weren't going to be in place to pick your child up, then you should have had a fucking back up plan.

A white Range Rover whipped into the parking lot, quickly coming to a halt in front of the steps. This guy stepped out and my eyes embraced his frame. He was bright. Just how I liked my men since I had a milk-chocolate complexion. His beard was full, connecting to his mustache. His head was big, almost bigger than his body, but that wasn't a turn-off.

Brushing his hand across his jet-black waves, he rounded the truck and Stormie's eyes lit up as they landed on him. Mine sparkled, a little bit. This was the first time I ever laid eyes on him before and was wondering what he was doing here after school hours.

His jeans sagged a little bit and I peeped the gun resting in the front of them. Weapons weren't even permitted on the premises, but that didn't stop him from bringing one up there anyway.

"Blessed!" Stormie hopped from the step and ran full speed toward him. Leaning down, he scooped her up into his arms with her feet dangling. I didn't think the shit was safe with him having that gun on him. I was terrified the shit might go off and hurt either one of them.

Rising to my feet, I dusted off the back of my pencil skirt and neared them. His dark eyes landed on me, and I tucked my hair back behind my ear before saying, "You're late. You do know that school has been out over twenty minutes. What type of father leaves his child stranded at school?"

Planting Stormie on her feet, he opened up the passenger's door and she climbed inside. Shutting the door, he turned to me. "Stormie isn't my child. Her father was running late and asked me to pick her up. If you got a problem, then you need to take that shit up with him."

He went to walk off, but I grabbed his wrist, stopping him. "Do you think it's safe for you to bring that with you up here? She shouldn't be around stuff like that."

"It's on me; it's not lying around where she can get her hands on it. Plus, it's on safety anyway. You really think I'd put my niece in danger like that?" His brow rose and he pulled away from me.

"The next time you come to pick her up, leave that at home," I told him, slowly backing away.

"You want to tell me how to wash my ass too?" The corner of his lip curved into a smirk.

"I was just suggesting for the safety of others. It's your choice to listen to me or not."

"I'm good," was all he said before jumping back into his truck and pulling off.

∞∞∞

Later that day...

"I'm sorry, I'm late," I told Sapphire as I rushed into *Kissed* hair salon. She was already in the chair getting her hair sewed by Gabby. I jumped into the chair alongside her and stared down at the KissedbyRyy deep wave pack. It was the only hair brand that Sapphire used.

"What took you so long anyway?" She brought her eyes up from her phone and cut them at me.

"I was stuck at school with one of my students. I really

can't understand why people can't be on time to pick their fucking children up. It's not like they get out different times every day or something." Shaking my head, I pulled my phone out of my Birkin and went straight to Facebook. People always talked about how toxic as fuck that little blue application was, but that motherfucker gave me life. I saw some of the funniest shit ever on there. If it wasn't for the laughs, I probably wouldn't even get on there.

"You know how people are." Sapphire shook her head and Gabby snatched it back. "Don't be pulling on my motherfucking head like that!" she snapped. I wasn't sure what I was going to do with that girl.

"Do you know what you're getting today?" Gabby asked me and I shrugged. I had been thinking about hairstyles all week long and couldn't figure out what I wanted. Every month, Sapphire and I would meet up at *Kissed* to get our hair done. And every two weeks, we meet to get our nails done. It was like a ritual of ours. We'd been doing it ever since we were back in high school.

Sapphire and I had been friends for what seemed like forever. That was my bitch and we damn near did everything together except fuck our niggas. I told her practically everything. She was my safe haven and vice versa.

When we were back in school, motherfuckers used to get mad as fuck at our bond. Hoes tried to come between us, but weren't successful.

"Do you ever know what the hell you want?" Sapphire questioned me.

"I'll figure it out by the time she's done with your hair. What happened to that wedding the other day? You usually call and let me know how it went, but I didn't hear anything from you."

Sapphire rolled her eyes. "I don't even want to talk about

that shit."

"Was it that bad?"

"You remember Jonathan, I was talking to?"

"What about him?" I set my phone down in my lap, giving her my undivided attention.

"That nigga was the fucking groom."

"What!" Gabby chimed in. She was nosy as hell, but we never had to worry about what we said leaving this room. A lot of our venting happened in these very chairs.

"Yes." Sapphire shook her head again. "I told Sherry about it and she called the wedding off. Her brother didn't seem too pleased with me about it though."

"Why the fuck do you care?"

"I don't, but that nigga was fine as fuck though. I wouldn't mind climbing that tree."

We both burst out laughing.

"That nigga was fine who picked my student up today, but I don't think I'd waste my time with his ass though."

"Why not?"

"He just rubbed me the wrong way."

Quickly, I snatched my phone up and went back to Face-book. I low-key wanted to see him again, but I didn't feel like wasting my time on another useless ass relationship. My last relationship didn't turn out too well. Christopher was every-thing... or at least I thought he was until I found him sneaking into a hotel room with another bitch. The shit wasn't even fuck-ing intentional. Sapphire was hosting an event at this hotel and when I got there, I found him with some hoe. I didn't understand what made him go out and cheat on me in the first place. Every-thing seemed fine in our relationship from my point of view.

"You good?" Sapphire asked me, bringing me back from my thoughts.

"Yeah, just have a lot on my mind," I told her.

"Do you want to talk about it?"

I shook my head. "It's nothing new. Just old bullshit that crossed my mind."

Gabby turned Sapphire around where she faced the mirror, so she could see the finished product. As always, she was bomb as fuck and Sapphire looked gorgeous as hell.

"Thanks." She grinned, whipped some cash out of her purse and handed it over to Gabby. Rising to my feet, I took the seat Sapphire once occupied and told Gabby, "I just want a straight sew-in."

"Really? It took you that long to come up with that shit?" Sapphire snickered at me and I gave her the bird finger.

"I just want something simple this time."

"Have it your way." She slouched down in the chair alongside me and I sat there, lost in my thoughts as Gabby began to remove my previous sew-in from my head.

Sapphire

A week later...

"**I** could probably schedule you a week from now. Let me take a look at my calendar," I spoke into my company iPhone as I scrolled through the calendar of my personal phone. "Yeah, it looks like I have a—" My sentence was cut short by the bursting of my office door. Sasha rushed in behind Sherry's brother as he burst in unannounced. My eyes cut to him and a frown rested on my face. I hated whenever people barged into my shit without knocking. It let me know that they lacked respect, and I couldn't deal with motherfuckers that were ill-mannered.

"I have an opening. I'll get my assistant to give you a call back and set everything up. I have to handle something right quick."

"Okay, thanks," the female said and hung up the phone.

"Why the fuck you barging in my shit like that?"

"You know your mouth foul as fuck for you to be a business woman."

Tell me something I don't know.

I waved Sasha off and she shut the door behind her. "What are you doing in my office?"

He neared my desk and my heart rate quickened. I tightly

pressed my thighs together to stop myself from leaking. His eyes were hidden by these expensive ass shades. He wasn't too skinny, but also wasn't that muscular. If I had to say, he was the perfect size. I was certain he'd be able to pick me up and all this ass with no hesitations.

Unlike the first time I laid eyes on him, he was dressed down in a simple black t-shirt and some denim jeans. From the gun tucked in the front of his pants, I knew he was nothing but trouble, but that still didn't push me away from wanting him. The things I wanted to do to this man was fucking unexplainable.

A loud thud noise brought me back from my thoughts. I gazed down at the duffel sitting on top of my desk. It was a couple of inches away from sitting on top of my fucking Mac Book. If he had hit my shit, he was coming out of the fucking pocket for a brand new one.

"What's this?"

Pulling his shades off his face, my eyes locked with his black ones, and he said, "I need you to clear your schedule for the next couple of weeks and plan a surprise birthday party for me."

I laughed because I didn't take this nigga serious.

"What's funny?" he quizzed with a raised brow.

"You are." Tears filled my eyes from laughing so hard.

"But I'm serious."

"Can't be. How you going to walk your ass in here and tell me what to do? I have plenty clients on my schedule over the next couple of weeks. What makes you think I'm just going to cancel on them to please you?"

"Maybe this will help you get a better understanding."

He unzipped the bag, opening it wide enough for me to

see inside. My eyes expanded when I saw all the Benjamins in there. I don't think I've ever seen that much money at one time before.

"What's that for?"

"I'll pay you whatever to make this shit happen and for it to be one of the best fucking events you've ever thrown before. You think you can make that happen for me?"

I chewed on the inside of my jaw, debating on what I wanted to do. If I accepted his proposal, this could be good on my resume, but the downfall would be me possibly losing clients. I already had to work twice as hard after Sherry's wedding. I didn't need for him to come in here and fuck me up even more.

"I don't think I could just cancel on clients. Some of them have been on the books for months. I can't afford to just let them go and lose business just because you want me to do something for you, but what I can do is make yours a priority and personally work on it myself. How does that sound to you?"

"Think I can work with that."

"Good. So, tell me what you want." I gestured for him to take a seat across from me in one of the chairs. He sat down and rattled off what he wanted done. It was basically nothing really. I hated whenever people came into my office and wanted me to throw an event for them and they didn't know what they wanted, but I'd been doing the shit for over six years now, and was able to pull off something amazing from little to no detail and somehow, it turned out to be exactly what they wanted in the first place.

By the end of the discussion, I concluded that he was throwing the party for his girl. I can't say I wasn't disappointed because I certainly was. I don't know why I thought someone as handsome as him would be single. After what happened with Jonathan, I needed to steer clear of men to avoid the shit ever happening again, but I wasn't sure if I'd be able to do just that. A bitch had needs and someone was going to have to take care of that shit soon rather than later.

"Okay, I'll see what I can do," I told him, rising to my feet and extending him my hand. I noted how his eyes caressed my thick frame and a smile overtook his face.

"Can't wait to see what you do." He firmly shook my hand and electricity coursed through it, pumping my heart. I quickly snatched it away, wiping my hand on my pants. My body was deceiving me. It knew this man was taken, but that didn't stop it from yearning for his touch. "Just remember, shit don't have no limit, so just go crazy."

"Will do." I flaunted him a nervous grin and he tread for the office door. "Hey!" I stopped him in his tracks, and he turned, facing me. "What's your name? I never caught it."

"Kon."

"Well, I'm Sapphire and I can't wait to work with you." Smirking, he left out of my office. Soon as the door closed, I released the breath, I didn't even know I was holding in.

∞∞∞

Later that day...

After spending almost the entire day in the office, trying to get a jump start on the party Kon wanted me to throw for him, my stomach grumbled and I knew it was time to stop by somewhere and grab me something to eat. Normally, I'd cook something or toss something in my crock pot before work, but since I didn't feel like going home and cooking anything, I stopped at one of the local seafood restaurants and grabbed something.

It didn't take me long. I was in and out of there. The aroma of crab legs brewed in my car, making me hungrier than I already was, and I couldn't wait to make it home to smash my food. Pulling into my driveway, I grabbed my food and purse and climbed out of the car.

As I sauntered up to the front door, I heard a car behind me and swiftly turned to see who it was. With me living alone, it had me paranoid most times. Especially with everything that was going on in the world today. I wasn't about to let anyone catch me slipping and I end up on the fucking news as a missing person.

When I saw the Benz sitting on the side of the street, I automatically knew who it was—Jonathan. I don't know what he was doing at my house. I thought it was pretty obvious that shit between us was over since he got his raggedy ass busted at the wedding. Whatever he had to say, I didn't feel like hearing the shit. All I wanted to do was go in there and eat my fucking crab legs in peace and soak in my tub with a nice bottle of wine.

"What are you doing here?" I asked him as he rounded his car and walked up into my yard.

"You ruined my fucking wedding and just walked away like it wasn't shit." He stopped directly in front of me and his Tom Ford cologne seeped up my nostrils. He purposely wore that scent for me. I had fallen head over hills in love with that shit and made sure to keep him a supply for whenever he came over. That shit instantly got my pussy throbbing every single time.

"That shit was so long ago. Don't tell me you're still in your fucking feelings about that shit." Turning, I unlocked my door and pushed it open. His hand swiftly wrapped around my waist and I felt him press him body up against me.

"Nah, I'm not mad."

"So, what the fuck are you doing here?"

His mouth eased toward the back of my neck and the hairs stood up. This nigga knew what the fuck he was doing, and I hated he caught me in such a vulnerable state. Any other nigga that tried to play me, I kicked their ass to the curb quicker than they could fucking blink. I hadn't had any dick since the last time we fucked, and he was trying to downplay my fucking emotions.

"You know exactly why I'm here." My pussy tingled a little bit and I quickly pulled away from him, stepping into the house.

"I'm not about to go there with you, Jonathan. You lied to me for fucking months and it's fucked up how you did Sherry. She didn't deserve that shit."

"Well, she damn sure doesn't want anything else to do with me now." He shut the door behind him. I should've put him out of my house, but I couldn't find it in myself to do so.

Setting my food down on the coffee table, I kicked my pumps off, popping my toes, and plopped down on the couch. Just because he was standing in my face, trying to fucking tempt me, didn't mean I wasn't going to eat my food. I had been waiting to devour my shit and I wasn't about to let him, nor his dick stand in the way.

"And you're crying to me because?" The last thing I wanted to hear was his problems that he caused in his own fucking relationship. When he laid down with someone other than his fiancée, he should have known that the shit was going to come back and bite him in the ass. If he was looking for me to feel sorry for him, then he was barking up the wrong tree.

My mouth watered as I opened my plate and my food stared back at me.

"I'm just saying... you owe me."

I damn near choked on my crab leg hearing that bullshit

seep from his lips.

"You're joking, right?" My eyes darted to him and he gazed at me with a stern expression.

"Does it look like I'm fucking joking?" Nearing me, he occupied the seat next to me on the couch and I ignored his ass. He could sit there and watch me suck the meat out of those crab legs, but I damn sure wasn't about to put my mouth on anything else just because he thought I fucking owed him something. I didn't owe anyone a got damn thing.

"Whatever Jonathan."

Gripping my feet, he pulled them up into his lap, causing me to place my plate in my lap and turn toward him. A moan escaped my lips when his fingertips deeply pressed into the sole of my foot. It had been forever since someone had massaged my damn feet. The closest I've come to a massage was when Ling did my feet every two weeks.

"Why are you trying to suck up to me right now?"

"I miss you, Sapphire," he said with a grin.

"I'm sure you do."

He had called me after the wedding, but I thought it was because he wanted to go off on me about getting the shit canceled.

"You gon' stop playing games with me?" He brought my right foot up to his lips and kissed the bottom of it.

"We'll see."

Dropping my foot, he slid over on the couch between my legs.

"You know you miss me too."

His fingers intertwined into my hair and his lips embraced the corner of my mouth. I was sure the special sauce was all over my mouth. I was never the type of person that was shy to eat around other people. I'll fuck some food up like a nigga and dare someone to say some shit.

"Where you going with this because right now, I'm not fucking moved."

"I swear I hate that reckless mouth of yours."

"Yet, you keep coming back."

Finishing up my crab legs, I set my plate on the table, giving him my undivided attention. As I ate, I was able to ignore my urge to fuck him because all I could think about was my food from the smell. Now that I was no longer eating, his cologne was damn near suffocating me.

"If the pussy wasn't so good..." he bit the corner of his lower lip and my pussy damn near surged.

His lips collided with mine and I crashed back against the arm of the couch. He snuggled between my legs. His dick pressed against my pelvis and that motherfucker was hard as a rock.

"You still tryna say you didn't miss me?" I grinned up at him and he unbuttoned my pants.

Pulling my pants and panties down, he tossed them to the floor and lifted me by the hips. His tongue swiftly went across his lips as he gazed down at my bald pussy. That was one thing about me, I hated having hair in places it wasn't supposed to be and loved my man man's dick to be shaved. I wouldn't let him enter me or even go down on him if he had hair. That shit was such a fucking turn off to me.

His lips caressed my clit and my eyes rolled to the back of my head. Jonathan gave some of the best head I've ever encountered. Maybe that was the reason why I kept him around so long and was pissed off that he had been lying to me.

I ground my pussy against his mouth. My toes curled and I gripped the couch, feeling my climax nearing. His tongue swiftly flicked against my clit and my body trembled underneath his fingertips.

His grip grew tighter as he held me in place.

"Fuuuuck!" I cried out as my orgasm washed over me.

He sucked all of my juices up and leaned back with my nectar, glistening on his mouth. I laughed, pressing my thighs together. He went to undo his belt, but I stopped him. I'd gotten mine; I saw no other use for him being here.

"What?" he asked with a raised brow.

"You can go now."

"Are you fucking serious?" He stood to his feet and mugged me.

"Yup. You know where the door is." Getting up, I grabbed my clothes up off the floor and stood to my feet.

"I'm not leaving here until I get what I came for."

"Yes, you are." Sauntering over to the door, I pulled it open and waited for him to get the fuck out of my house.

"No." Stopping directly in front of me, he grabbed my wrist and I pulled away from him.

"Goodbye Jonathan, and don't bring your ass back here."

His jaw muscles tightened as he gazed back at me. I knew he was angry as fuck about me using him, but that's actually what he'd been doing the last few months we were messing around. He couldn't get mad about me doing him the same way.

"Fuck you." He stormed out of there and I shut the door behind him. I was full and got an awesome orgasm. Once I finished my shower, I was going to sleep like a baby.

Blessed Thomas

The next day...

Turning over in bed, a smile graced my face as I stared at the chocolate beauty I picked up at the club the night before. That wasn't unusual for me. If I saw something I liked, I went after the shit at all costs, and women were no exception.

Some might think of me as a player, but I didn't really think that was the case. I just found myself getting bored with women and moved on to the next. It was hard as fuck for a woman to grasp and hold my attention.

Gently shaking her, I woke her from her slumber. She served her purpose last night and now it was time for her to go. If I wasn't so fucking wasted the night before, I would have sent her ass on her way then. I rarely let women spend the night with me. My trust was thin as fuck when it came to anyone other than Kon.

That nigga was really the only family I had around this motherfucker. He was the only person I trusted with my got damn life and I didn't think the shit would ever change.

"Good morning." She grinned from ear to ear.

"Don't you have to go to work or something?"

Her face scrunched up. "Is that your way of kicking me out or something?"

"I gotta get up and get ready for work," I quickly lied. I didn't plan on doing a damn thing today, but she didn't need to know all that. What I wasn't about to do was sit at home and entertain her ass.

"Okay."

Without saying another word, she got up from the bed and my eyes zeroed in on that fat ass as it bounced as she entered the bathroom. I heard the shower running and assumed she was going to take a quick one before heading out.

My phone vibrated on the nightstand, grasping my attention. Glancing over, I saw Kon calling me. I swiftly scooped the phone up and swiped it.

"What's up?"

"Did I wake you?"

"Nah, I been up for a little bit. Something's wrong?"

"I have to go take care of some shit this morning, but Stormie has a field trip and Chrissy can't take off. I was wondering if you could take my place?"

I loved Stormie as if she was my own. I'd do anything when it came to that little girl, but I wasn't sure if I wanted to spend my day with that rude ass, know it all teacher of hers and a bunch of kids.

"I guess I can do that."

"You sure? If you can't make it, then I can just call and let them know that something came up."

"Nah, you know I'd do anything for her. What time should I be there?"

"I was supposed to be at the school ten minutes ago. I can call them right quick and let them know that someone is on their way."

"Okay."

The call disconnected and I climbed out of the bed. Water was still running in the bathroom and I got up to see what the hell shorty had going on. Pushing the door open, I saw her standing in the mirror with a towel wrapped around her and my toothbrush shoved into her mouth.

"What the fuck are you doing?"

She jumped at the sound of my voice.

"Brushing my teeth." She mumbled, spitting into the sink.

"With my got damn toothbrush!"

"Yeah." She shrugged and I wanted to smash her fucking head into the got damn mirror.

"Hurry up and get the fuck out of my house!"

This bitch was overstepping her got damn boundaries. I didn't know shit about this motherfucker, and she wanted to use my got damn toothbrush. Who the fuck does shit like that?

Rolling her eyes, she tossed my toothbrush onto the counter and bumped me as she left out of the bathroom. I turned the shower back on and grabbed me a brand-new toothbrush head out of the cabinet. After handling my hygiene, I went back into my bedroom to get dressed. The nasty bitch was gone, and I was happy as fuck too. That bitch was going to get her got damn head knocked the fuck off if she kept playing with me.

I quickly tossed something on and headed out of the door. Since I was going to be around children for most of the day, I decided to leave my gun at home and not because that teacher lady told me to.

Hopping into my car, I rushed to the school. Pulling into the parking lot, I saw the two school buses sitting in front of the building. Stormie's teacher paced back and forth between the two with her phone shoved up to her face. Clearly, she was frustrated about me getting there late, but it wasn't my fault. Kon called me late as hell and knew I had to take a shower and shit.

Climbing out of the car, I tread up to where she stood with her back facing me. "Let's get this show on the road," I said, and she jumped with her hand covering her chest.

"Why you sneaking up on me?" She slipped her phone into her purse and neared the first bus. "I really wish y'all would be on time when it comes to Stormie."

"Shit ain't my fault. He called me this morning and asked me to cover for him."

"Lucky for us, I was able to call the Aquarium to let them know we were running late."

Stepping onto the bus behind her, my eyes landed on all the children that were in there. I wasn't the best when it came to children, but I did damn well dealing with Stormie.

"Blessed!" Stormie jumped from her seat and rushed up to me almost knocking me over. I scooped her up into my arms and pecked her on the cheek.

"Now that our chaperone is here, we can get going."

The children clapped and screamed damn near piercing my eardrums. I was beginning to think this shit was a fucking mistake, letting Kon talk me into this bullshit. Planting Stormie on her feet, I told her, "Go back to your seat."

Nodding, she ran down the aisle and sat down alongside Ember, one of her friends. I knew who she was because I'd picked them up on different occasions and dropped them off at home. I wasn't the friendly type of person and had told Stormie several times to watch who she befriended. Those little motherfuckers may act like they were your friends, but would turn on you with the quickness. Then Kon and I would be ripping the fucking school apart trying to figure out who the hell hurt her. It was best for everyone for her to not be so got damn friendly.

The teacher took a seat at the front of the bus and I slouched down in the one directly behind her, sitting sideways. I couldn't even remember the last time my ass graced a bus seat. Shit, when I was in high school, I drove myself back and forth to school. Whenever they went on those dumbass field trips, I stayed the fuck out the way. School wasn't for me. When Kon gave me the opportunity to join him and come up in the dope game, it was one of the best decisions I ever made.

The bus jerked and pulled out of the parking lot. Since I was going to be stuck with them for most of the day, I thought it would be nice to get to know the teacher.

"You never told me what your name was," I blurted, and she glanced in my direction and took her attention back to the book she was reading.

"You can call me Ms. Gates just like everyone else."

"Okay, then, Ms. Gates," I said with a smirk on my face. "Where are you from, Ms. Gates?" I eased up, resting my arms on the back of her seat. Strawberries crept up my nostrils and it made me want to inhale her hair even more.

"That's none of your business."

"You say that now, but I bet soon, I'll have you eating out the palm of my hand."

"Tuh," was her only response.

I'd fucked a lot of women in my day, but I don't think I've ever came across a teacher that was as fine as her, and that I wanted to fuck the shit out of. She had this gorgeous mocha skin complexion and long off-black hair. Her lips were full as fuck and all I could think about was them wrapped around my—

"Can you sit back in your seat?" she asked, not removing her eyes from her book.

"Can you stop being rude toward a nigga and let me get to know you?"

Swiftly turning around in her seat, she faced me with a scowl. "Stop using that foul language. I don't want my students going home telling their parents we be cursing around them."

I tossed my hands up in surrender. Me not cursing was going to be hard as hell, but I guess I could give it a try for her. "Fine."

I rested back against my seat and was quiet for the remainder of the ride. We pulled up to the Aquarium and the children got all hyped and shit. I didn't know what was supposed to be so special about going to see some damn fish trapped behind got damn glass.

"Settle down!" Ms. Gates rose to her feet and all the children immediately grew quiet. All their little beady eyes fell upon her. "We have to split you all up in groups. Pay attention because I will have a quiz on the fish tomorrow when you get to class. Don't wander off on your own or else you would be in big trouble. Let's go; starting with this side." She pointed to the left of her and all the children on that side stood to their feet. They climbed off the bus and waited for her and the rest of the children to get off as well.

I stepped to the side and watched as she separated the class. "This group... you'll be going with Blessed."

"Excuse me?" I damn near choked on my own saliva. She had ten children, standing there, gazing up at me. She had to have lost her fucking mind if she thought I was going to be able to handle that many fucking children by myself.

"What did you think you were coming along for?"

"Just to be here."

"All you have to do is make sure the children stay in the line while the guide takes you all around the Aquarium and gives them a lesson on the fish. It's not hard, Blessed."

This was the second time I wanted to kick my own fucking ass for agreeing with this shit.

"Alright, let's go. If anyone falls behind, you'll get left."

"Blessed!" she shouted behind me.

"I was just kidding." I chortled and led the group of children into the building. We were met by the tour guide soon as we stepped through the door.

"*Everly Elementary*?" she quizzed, approaching us.

"Yes."

"Okay, follow me this way."

The children filed behind her as I stepped into the back of the line where I'd be able to keep an eye on every single one of them. I was trying to get in good with Ms. Gates and knew I wouldn't be able to if I were to let something happen to one of those children.

We followed the woman around the building for two hours and then she took us into a room with the other groups of children. I saw Ms. Gates making her way through the dining hall with brown paper bag lunches and handing them out to the children. My group sat down at the last empty rectangular table as I posted up on the wall with my eyes trained on her.

I don't know what the fuck it was about her. Whether it was her looks, or how rude she was towards me, or how she didn't fall all over me like most women did, but I did know... I wanted Ms. Gates. I wanted her in the worst way imaginable and knew it was going to take everything inside me to acquire her, even if it was just for one night.

"Are you hungry?" Her voice brought me from my thoughts. She stood directly in front of me in the form-fitting black dress with a short split in the back. She wasn't all that curvy like most women I went for. That's another reason why I didn't understand how come I was craving her.

"What's in it?"

"Either you're hungry or you're not. Doesn't matter what's in the bag."

That was the shit I was talking about. That mouth of hers made me want to fuck her even more.

"I guess I can eat something."

She shoved the bag into my stomach and strutted off. My eyes locked in on her ass and I was pretty sure she knew it too because the motherfucker swayed a little bit harder. She took a seat at this small circular table by herself and pulled her book out of her purse, emptying the contents from her brown paper bag onto the table. I'm not certain what the hell she thought a sandwich, apple, and small bag of chips was going to do to a nigga like me, but to make her happy, I was going to eat the shit. When I got back to the school, I was flying somewhere and grab me some real food.

I stood there, watching her take a bite of her sandwich and smile at something she was reading. That smile was everything. The motherfucker was perfect with those pearly whites. Peeling away from the wall, I strolled over to where she sat and occupied the chair directly in front of her.

"Did I say I wanted company?"

"Well, this was the only seat left."

"You were fine standing up."

"Let me ask you something." I snatched the book away from her and closed it. Her mouth fell ajar.

"You made me lose the page I was on."

"What do you have against me? You know absolutely nothing about me, yet you're always trying to push me away."

"I know men like you, and I honestly don't have time for it." She stuck her hand out, palm facing the ceiling. "Can I have my book back now?"

"What you mean, men like me?" She piqued my interest, and I wanted to know what she meant by that shit. I hated when people tried to fucking judge me without getting to know me first. This was her second time encountering me, and she thought she had me all mapped out in her pretty little head.

"When I say men like you, I mean men that see every woman and want to have sex with them. I won't be another notch on your belt."

"This your second time seeing me. How you figure that's what I'm about?"

"It's called woman's intuition babe, and mine is telling me to stay as far away from you as possible."

Yanking the book away from me, she went back to reading. I left her alone for the remainder of the trip, but that didn't mean I was going to give up. I had my eyes set on her, and I was going to get her ass whether she liked it or not.

Sapphire

A week later...

K on never told me what type of cake he wanted at the birthday party, so I set up a lunch to meet with him, so he could do a little cake tasting at Divine's Cakes where I mostly got all of my cakes from. This was going to be the first time I saw him since he barged into my office demanding shit. For all of our other affairs, we spoke over the phone and tried to keep shit brief between us.

My nerves were all over the place about this lunch. I found myself tossing clothes all over my bedroom this morning, trying to find the perfect outfit for the day. It literally took me over an hour to settle on this all-white pants suit with a navy-blue corset. The shit was bomb as fuck and I had my hair flowing down my back in spiral curls.

I watched the diamond studded clock on my wall in my office, waiting for the time to wind down, and I could run out of there and see Kon. I know it was wrong for me to be lusting over that man the way I was, but he was damn fine, and I just couldn't help myself. Ever since I saw him at the wedding, all I wanted to do was jump on that nigga's dick. If I was one of those home-wrecking bitches, I definitely would have shot my shot.

To me, Kon didn't really look like the type that would cheat on his girl. That was another thing that drew me to him. I know he engaged in a little eye candy every once in a while, because I noticed how he always eyed me whenever he was around.

Soon as the clock struck eleven, I hopped from my desk and grabbed my purse out of the bottom drawer. I was supposed to meet Kon at *Divine's* at eleven forty-five and I was going to make sure I was there and on time, waiting for him.

"Sasha, I'm heading out to meet a client," I told her when I stepped out the office.

"Do you want me to forward all your calls to your cell?"

"Just take a message. I don't want anything to interrupt my meeting."

Her brows arched as she eyed me. I didn't say anything else, just stepped on the elevator and got out of there.

It didn't take me long to make it to *Divine's*. When I arrived, Kon wasn't there, but I took my seat at a table anyway.

"Do you want something while you wait?" Doris asked me after I got comfortable.

"Can I have a glass of wine?"

"Sure." She went to the back and came back with my glass of wine. "Let me know if you need anything else."

Smiling, I turned my glass up and glanced out the window at all the people that were strolling by. My heart pounded in my chest as I sat there waiting for him to get there.

Ten minutes had passed, and I was beginning to think he wasn't going to show. I thought about calling him to see where he was, but I opted out of it. I didn't want him to think I was desperate or anything, so I was going to give him twenty more minutes before I decided to get up and leave. This nigga wanted me to make him a fucking priority, but he couldn't even make it to a fucking meeting on time.

Grabbing my phone, I pulled up my social medias to make

sure they were still running properly. Since I was busy most of the day, Sasha would be the one making my posts. Of course, I had to approve them first before she posted anything.

The door chimed and I looked up. Kon strolled into the building and my panties instantly grew moist. Just as the last time I saw him, he was so got damn fine. Pulling his shades from his face, he took a seat in front of me.

"I thought you weren't coming."

"Sorry, I was running a little late. I'm here now, so let's get this shit started." Lifting his hand, he beckoned for Doris and she hurried over to the table.

"Are you ready to get started now?"

"Yes, you can bring out the samples," I told her, taking another sip from my wine, and he pulled my cup away from me and took a sip himself.

"They don't have anything stronger than this shit?"

"This is a bakery, not a fucking club, Kon." I snatched my wine away from him and sat it down on the table.

Doris came back with at least ten different cake samples and sat them down on the table in front of us.

"Do we really have to try this much cake? I'm not into sweets like that."

"What's Chrissy's favorite flavor? Maybe we could use that instead of tasting different ones."

"I don't know."

"How you don't know your girlfriend's favorite cake?" My brow arched. "What's her favorite color?"

"I don't know... pink, I think."

"Do you know anything about this girl? Did you just meet her or something?"

"No, we've been together for over nine years. We have a daughter together and everything." Picking up a fork, he toyed with a piece of vanilla cake to keep himself from locking eyes with me. If they had been together for that long, then he should have known every single detail about her like the back of his hand.

I used to envy relationships that lasted that long until I found out most of them weren't even happy in their own relationship. Some of them were getting abused and hiding the shit. Some were getting cheated on constantly, but didn't want to let go of the relationship because it was all they knew, and they died to be with their significant other.

"How about this one?" I shoved the strawberry cake over in front of him and his face scrunched up. "Just try it."

I sat there and watched him dig the fork into the cake and shove it into his mouth. I don't know what the fuck was going on with me, but I could have sworn he did that shit in slow motion and my pussy began to tingle.

Clearing my throat, I tightly pressed my thighs together and shifted in my seat.

"It's alright."

"Okay, so strawberry is off the list."

I gazed down at the different variety of tiny square cakes and chewed on the inside of my jaw, debating on which one I wanted him to try. I definitely didn't want to be in there all fucking day, playing over cake. I'm sure he had other shit to do, so I wanted to get this handled in a fashionable manner.

"Try this one; it's my personal favorite." I eased the double chocolate fudge cake over in front of him and he gazed down at it.

He dug the fork down into the cake and took a bite. I observed as he chewed and noticed the corner of his mouth curve into a smirk.

"It's good, huh?" I grinned, stealing a piece with my own fork. The chocolate melted into my mouth, and I moaned. I absolutely loved that cake. Almost every time I was in there, I'd get Doris to get me a slice to take home.

Opening my eyes, I saw Kon staring directly at me. A smile passed his lips, and I realized I might have sounded a little dirty, moaning after eating that cake. My face flushed.

"It is really that good?" He dipped his finger into the fudge and shoved it toward my mouth. My teeth sank into the corner of my lower lip before I sucked it off his fingertip.

"It really is. So, what do you—" Before I could finish my sentence, the door chimed and my eyes darted toward it. Some chick mugged me and stormed over to our table. She was beautiful, to say the least, but that scowl on her face made her ugly as hell.

Her body was stacked, but it wasn't anything compared to me. Her complexion was bright, and her hair stopped at her shoulders. I wasn't certain if it was a lace front or her actual hair, but either way, I didn't give a damn. The way she was eyeing me was pissing me the fuck off. If she knew what was best for her, she'd take her ass on about her business.

"Nigga, I thought you were supposed to be at the warehouse! Who the fuck is this!" Her eyes shifted to Kon, and it was then that I knew she had to be his girlfriend.

"Will you chill the fuck out?" His facial expression went from a smile to annoyed real quick.

"No! I won't chill the fuck out! Answer my got damn question! Who the fuck is this hoe!" Kon gripped her hand, but she snatched away from him. "I knew you were fucking cheating on me!" Tears filled her eyes and I just sat there, anticipating how this was going to play out. She didn't know what the hell was going on and jumping to conclusions.

"Ain't nobody fucking cheating on your ass." He rose to his feet and she peeped around at me.

"The fuck you looking at, hoe?"

"Wait a minute." A smile slipped onto my face and I stood as well. I didn't have a damn thing to do with her issues with Kon, but I damn sure wasn't about to sit there and let her fucking disrespect me. "I suggest you handle this shit, Kon, or she going to be lying on that fucking floor, and you going to have to carry her ass out of here."

"Your ass out here with my man, and think you're going to whoop my ass?" She laughed and poked herself in the chest.

"You disrespect me again, and I am going to whoop your ass."

"Hoe!"

I lunged toward her and Kon caught me before I was able to drag that fucking bitch. I was never the one to do all that talking. If my mama didn't teach me anything else, she taught me to swing on a bitch first.

"So, you're taking up for this ho now? You love her?"

"Will you just tell this delusional bitch who I am before she gets her ass kicked?"

As Kon held me in his arms, I inhaled his intoxicating scent. I didn't want him to release me, but I knew that was going to happen as soon as dummy found out he wasn't cheating on her with me. She was lucky as fuck I didn't try to take his ass away from her. It seemed like to me, he didn't want to be there in the first place.

"For the last time, I'm not fucking cheating on you. I hired Sapphire to plan an event. We were in here tasting fucking cake." She glimpsed at the cake on the table and her bright face flushed.

She was embarrassed as fuck for coming in there and acting the way she was.

Kon released me and I was highly disappointed. I wanted to be in his presence a little bit longer. Something in me told me he was going to leave with her and there was no telling when I was going to be able to see him again.

"Let me get her out of here before these people don't allow us to come back." He shoved Chrissy toward the door, and I stopped him.

"What about the cake? You never told me which one you wanted."

"That chocolate one is fine."

"Okay, if I need anything else, I'll just let you know."

He and Chrissy disappeared out of the door. They were still arguing as he pulled her toward a car.

"Are you okay?" Doris asked me when she came back.

"I'm fine. We're going to stick with this one."

"What type of frosting?"

Kon and I didn't make it that far and I didn't think it was necessary to call him and ask about something as silly as frosting, so I was just going to make the choice for him and pray for the best.

"Whipped, white and gold."

"I'll let you know when I have the first design ready."

Nodding, I gathered my things and left out of the store.

"I really don't feel up to it," I told Sa'nai through the

phone, tossing myself on the bed.

"Come on, Sapphire. I know you had a long day, and this is exactly what you need right now."

"Actually, the complete opposite."

For the last ten minutes, she had been trying to persuade me into going to some stupid ass club opening. I wasn't really in the mood. All I wanted to do was eat and binge watch a show on Netflix or Hulu.

"I promise it'll be fun."

I looked up and Sa'nai was strutting into my bedroom already dressed to go to the club as if she just knew I was going to tell her yes.

"Remind me to take my key from you." Hanging up the phone, I gave her my undivided attention. "I'm just not in the clubbing mood."

Dropping her clutch on the bed, she went over to my walk-in closet and began going through my clothes.

"After the week I've had, I deserve this shit and you know I'm not going to go out alone." That was our system. We never went out alone and whenever we went out, we always made sure the other got home safely no matter how fucking drunk we were. I was never the type of person that got so drunk and couldn't tell you what happened the night before. I was conscious as a motherfucker. If something happened while I was drunk, it happened because I wanted it to.

She tossed a blue bodycon dress onto the bed and went back into the closet to go and find some shoes to match.

"You're going to the club with me, so you might as well get your ass up and get in the tub."

Entering the bathroom, she started the shower. This motherfucker wasn't going to give up until I got up out of that bed and got dressed.

"Let's go. The water should be nice and hot by now."

She tugged on my arm, pulling me up from the bed. "Do I really have to?" I whined, dragging my feet toward the bathroom.

"Yes, you do. I'll be right out here, waiting for you with the hair wand and makeup." She smacked me on the ass and shoved me into the bathroom, shutting the door.

Taking a deep breath, I stripped out of my clothes and stepped over into the walk-in shower. Forty minutes later, I climbed out, wrapping the towel around my waist and brushed my teeth.

"Hurry up in there!" she shouted through the door.

"I'm coming!" I mumbled, spitting the toothpaste out in the sink and rinsed my mouth out.

I tread back into the room and found me a bra and panties set. I took my time lotioning my body and getting dressed, thinking she was just going to give up and leave, but I was wrong. Gripping me by the shoulders, she pushed me down on the bench at my vanity and went to work on my hair.

"I know you keep saying that you don't want to go, but I'm sure you're going to have a ball when we get there."

"That's what your mouth says now."

When she finished my hair and makeup, I stepped to the floor-length mirror to get a good look at how everything had turned out. I was cute. The dress sat my breasts up perfectly and hugged every single curve. My hair was in a half up and half down curly style and she had done my makeup to perfection.

"You look damn good. Let's go. Our Uber is outside waiting for us." She yanked me away from the mirror and I grabbed my purse on the way out the door. Luckily for me, inside my Birkin, I kept a crossbody Fendi. It had all my essentials inside in case I wanted to make a run to the store or something and didn't want to carry that huge purse with me. People thought that they were slick and would try to grab your shit with the quickness. I wasn't the one they were going to catch slipping.

Grabbing the crossbody, I dropped the Birkin on the couch and locked up the house behind us.

It didn't take us long to make it to this new club called *Nova Beach*. It sat right on the beach with the perfect view of the ocean. I had heard about them starting the club, but I didn't have any intentions on coming to the grand opening.

We climbed out of the car and saw that the fucking line was damn near wrapped around the building. I'm not certain why the hell she wanted to decide to come here on opening night like we had some reservations or some shit.

Sometimes we were lucky enough to persuade the bouncer to let us jump the line, then there were other times when the bouncer was a complete asshole and we had to stand in them. That was something I hated about going out. If I had thrown an event at the club before, they would welcome us with open arms, but seeing how this one was new and I had no idea of who owned it, we had a fifty-fifty chance of getting into the door without any problems.

"Do you see this fucking line?" I asked her as we approached it.

"I didn't think it was going to be this long. We would have gotten here earlier if you had just got up when I first told you to."

"Oh, so now you trying to blame this shit on me? I told you I was perfectly fine being at home in my bed."

"Let's try our luck."

We neared the door and Sa'nai flashed the bouncer a bright smile. Her smile was one of her best assets.

"Name?" he asked, glancing down at the clipboard in his hand. If they were allowing people inside based on that list, there's no way we were making it through that door.

"Sa'nai Gates." Clasping her hands together, she leaned over, trying to get a peep at the list, but he moved it out of her sight. I already knew what she was trying to do. She knew her name wasn't going to be on the list, so she was going to steal someone's name to use for me. We were wasting our fucking time, trying to get into that club.

"You're not on the list."

"Are you sure? Can you look again?"

"And this is why we should turn around and go back home," I suggested, but Sa'nai was determined to get into that club.

"What about you?" He turned his attention to me.

"Sapphire Snow."

I nibbled on the corner of my lower lip as I watched him skim the list for my name that I knew wasn't going to be on there.

"Go ahead." He nodded toward the door.

"Are you serious?" Sa'nai's eyes expanded. I was just as shocked as she was.

He gazed at us, but didn't utter another word. Gripping Sa'nai's hand, I pulled her toward the entrance before he changed his mind.

"You mind telling me how the hell you got on that fucking list?" she quizzed, pointing her thumb over her shoulder.

"The hell if I know."

We entered the club and they had this ocean-blue theme going on. It was beautiful. Instead of having regular barstools, they were made out of swings. The bar was completely glass with water inside it and exotic fish.

Sa'nai pulled me straight to the bar. It was the entire point in her coming out, so she could get drunk. If I was going to be stuck there with her, I knew that I was going to have to have a few drinks myself.

Climbing onto the swing, she waved her hand in the air to grab the bartenders' attention. I eased down on the one alongside her, gently swinging back and forth.

The bartender finally made it to our end of the bar. She had on this cute yellow one-piece swimsuit that was cut out on the sides. Her hair flowed in nice huge curls and the smile she wore was even larger.

"What can I get for you!" she shouted over the loud music, but I heard her perfectly.

"Give us each four shots of Patrón," Sa'nai told her. I would have objected to that idea, but I needed all the liquor in my system where I'd end up having a good time and not drive her insane.

We quickly tossed our drinks back and the song changed. I wasn't sure who the artist was, but the beat was crazy. Sa'nai jumped from her swing, yanking me from mine in the process and ran out to the crowded dance floor. Putting her hands on her knees, she bent over, twerking her ass on me. I giggled because Sa'nai didn't have much ass, but that definitely didn't stop her from trying to twerk that shit. The effects of the liquor were brewing inside me. Sweat beads formed on my forehead. I let go to have fun.

We had been on the dance floor for three songs straight and Sa'nai was still dancing as if it was the first song. This girl had so much fucking energy to burn. I didn't understand how when she dealt with children all week long. You'd think she would have been drained.

Cologne wrapped around my head before I felt a firm body press up against me from behind. I was used to men trying to shoot their shot whenever I went out and I always politely turned their asses down. I encountered all sorts of men and most of them weren't really my type. They tried their hardest to pretend they were someone they weren't, and that shit was a huge turn off to me.

Spinning around, I fixed my mouth to say something, but my words got caught in my throat when I realized who was standing behind me. He gazed down into my eyes and my pussy immediately grew wet. He had been on my mind the entire day since our meeting at Divine's earlier. I thought about texting to check on him and see how he was doing with Chrissy, but that wasn't professional, and I was trying my best to keep shit professional between us no matter how much I wanted to fuck him.

"What are you doing here!" I shouted over the music.

Gripping my hand, he started to pull me away, but I wasn't about to leave Sa'nai out there on that dance floor alone. She had a couple more drinks and I knew I was going to have to keep an eye on her. Quickly catching her hand, I pulled her behind me. I could feel her stumbling over her own feet as she tried to keep up with us.

I wasn't sure where he was taking me, but I was so stuck in his trance that I didn't really give a fuck. Maybe he wanted to talk to me about the party he had me planning. But then I thought about how he damn near pressed that third leg all up and between my ass cheeks not too long ago. Kon was confusing as fuck and his bitch was crazy as hell, so I didn't need to be around him too fucking long. Fighting that bitch wasn't in the plans for the night. I came out with Sa'nai to take my mind off things.

Kon led us up to a VIP section on the second floor. There weren't many people in there—a couple of guys and like five girls. I'm sure they were trying their best to get a come up around here. The type of money I was sure Kon and his friends had was endless.

The music wasn't as loud on the second floor. Releasing my hand, he took a seat on the blue plush couch and grabbed a bottle of Hennessey, turning it straight up. I stood there, chewing on the inside of my jaw, wondering exactly why he brought me up there.

"Wha-what are you doing here?" I glanced back at Sa'nai and she was staring at this guy sitting on the couch with a girl on either side of him. I'd never seen him around before and it made me wonder exactly how she knew him.

"Ms. Gates." A huge grin formed on his face as his eyes locked with hers.

Sa'nai placed her arm on my shoulder and leaned into my side, whispering, "That's the guy I told you about."

"The one you said was fine, but you didn't want to go there?"

She nodded and peeled away from my side.

"My intuition is never wrong." She neared where he sat and pulled one of the girls up from the couch. The girl's mouth fell agape as Sa'nai took her seat alongside the guy. For someone that didn't want him, she sure as hell wasn't acting like it.

"Are you going to sit down or just stand there?" Kon's low eyes landed on me. I was hesitant at first, but I eased over and took the seat alongside him.

"Why you brought me up here?"

"I saw you down there and thought we could talk."

"Oh, really? About what?" I shifted, getting comfortable on the couch and took the Hennessey bottle away from him, taking a swig.

"I wanted to apologize to you about earlier."

"You don't have to apologize about that. I know how women can get sometimes." I've never been in that predicament before. If I thought a nigga was cheating, I let his ass go and was done with the shit. If a nigga really wanted to be with you, then you wouldn't have to worry about someone else taking your fucking spot. He'd do all he could to make sure you knew you were his one and only. Some of these women be doing the fucking most and stressing themselves the fuck out for no got damn reason.

"But still, that bullshit wasn't called for."

"Are you two good?" Grabbing the bottle, he took a huge gulp from it.

"Even after we left, she was still arguing and shit. I had to let her ass go. She can't keep embarrassing me and shit like that."

His eyes danced out to the crowd underneath us. I felt sorry for him. To end a relationship that had that much history had to be difficult.

"I'm so sorry to hear that. I hope you didn't end things because of me." I was doing a little happy dance inside, knowing they were no longer together. I didn't know if they were going to get back with each other, but if he wanted to spend his time away from her with me, I wasn't going to complain about it.

"Nah, that shit's been a long time coming."

"What does that mean about the party then?"

"You might as well gon' and cancel that shit."

"Really?"

"After the way she been acting, she doesn't deserve a fucking party from me."

"I'll get right on it in the morning, but you'll still have to pay me for my services."

"I know."

Reaching into his pocket, he pulled a pre-rolled blunt out and tucked it between his lips, lighting the tip. I relaxed back in my seat and my eyes landed on Sa'nai. She was still sitting over there with that guy laughing and talking. I'm positive the only reason why was because she was fucking drunk.

After sitting there for a while, Kon and I had damn near finished that entire bottle of Hennessey and I was feeling fucking amazing. Sa'nai disappeared with that guy. If she didn't come back soon, I was going to go searching for her to make sure she was okay. She came there with me, so she was my responsibility.

A slow song came on, and I don't know what took over my body, but I found myself sitting in Kon's lap with my back facing him and grinding. His dick stiffened underneath me and my pussy throbbed. I haven't had any since the last time Jonathan showed up on my doorstep and he licked the pussy. I needed some fucking dick and now that he was freshly single, I wouldn't feel bad about seducing his sexy ass.

His fingertips brushed against my arms, causing goosebumps all over my skin. My teeth sank into my lower lip and I glanced back at him over my shoulder. His eyes were red and low as he gazed at me lustfully.

"Keep on and you gon' find that dick up in your ass."

"Promise?" The corner of my lips curved into a smirk.

Glancing around the section, I noticed we were the only ones in there. His massive hand gripped my thigh and eased up my dress. I moaned at the touch of his hand. I don't know if it was because I had been yearning for his touch for the longest or what.

Spreading my legs, I tilted my head back against his shoulder. His fingers gently massaged my clit through my panties. My eyes closed, and I nibbled on my lower lip, trying to fight back the moans that were threatening to seep through my lips.

"That pussy wet as fuck ain't it?"

"Mmhmm," I moaned, and he slipped his index finger into my panties, inserting it in my pussy.

"Wonder if it tastes good."

He sucked my juices off his finger and that shit drove me fucking crazy. Turning in his lap, I cupped his face and meshed our lips. My nectar intertwined with his Kush tasting tongue. Moans seeped through my lips and all I wanted to do was jump on his dick.

Straddling him, he lifted my dress up over my waist and shoved my panties to the side.

"Ungh!" I moaned as soon as I felt the tip of his dick enter me. My teeth snagged his lower lip as I tilted my head back. His dick filled me up perfectly.

Gripping his shoulders, I bounced up and down on his dick. This was the first time I ever did anything like that inside a club. I wasn't the type to have sex in crazy places, I've thought about it, but was too afraid to get caught doing something like that. The last thing I needed was something on my record that could affect my company. With Kon, all of that went out the window.

His lips embraced my neck, licking, kissing, and sucking. I felt my climax building up inside me. My eyes rolled to the back of my head and I released my juices. His hands snaked around, cupping my ass. I ground on his dick some more, not caring that my pussy was sensitive as hell.

"Fuck," he groaned in my ear. Hearing a nigga make noise during sex was the ultimate turn on.

Gripping me tightly by the waist, he held me still, releasing his seeds. I lifted off his dick and slid onto the couch alongside him. He stuffed his dick back down into his jeans.

"Kon!" Chrissy screamed before even making it into the

section. She wore a scowl as she charged toward us with two chicks behind her. "This the reason why you fucking broke up with me!" Her eyes darted to me, and I tugged on the bottom of my dress to make sure it was all the way down. I was so lost in Kon's trance that I didn't even know how long she had been standing there.

"Don't come up in here with that bullshit." He grabbed the Hennessey bottle and chugged the remainder of the liquor.

"Thought you said she was just a fucking event planner. What the fuck she doing up in here with you and shit!" She neared us and I shifted in my seat just in case I had to jump up and whoop her fucking ass.

"Take your ass to your section or go home," he told her without looking in her direction.

"I'm not going any fucking where!" Reaching across me, she mushed him in the head.

I shoved her arm back. She was all in my fucking personal space and I didn't play that shit. "You're too fucking close."

"So, what, bitch?" She poked me in the forehead with her stiletto nails and I slapped her hand down.

"Bitch, don't fucking touch me!" I shot straight to my feet prepared to give her the ass whooping she was looking for, not giving a damn she had two bitches with her. I'd try my best to whoop all of their asses if I had to.

Kon immediately stepped in between us probably sensing shit was about to get ugly. "Why are you coming up in here starting shit? You knew how much tonight meant for me. I'm not gon' ask you to take your ass back to your section again."

"You knew how much my relationship meant to me! That didn't stop your ass from fucking this bitch behind my back."

"Who the fuck you calling a bitch?" I shoved him, trying my best to get around to her ass. This bitch was pushing my fucking buttons.

"I'm talking to you, hoe! What, you couldn't go out and find your own man, so you had to fucking steal mine!" Tears filled her eyes. I didn't steal anyone. If Kon didn't want to be with her anymore, then it was her fucking fault, not mine.

Reaching into his pocket, he pulled his phone out and dialed a number. I sat back down on the couch because this bitch wasn't worth me losing my got damn cool over.

My head yanked to the side and it was then that I realized the bitch got past Kon and pulled me by my fucking hair.

"That's my fucking man!" she shouted as I rose to my feet. She snatched my shit so fucking hard that she pulled my fucking closure off.

"Bitch!" I was fuming now. Picking up one of the empty bottles off the table, I charged her ass with it. The bitches that were there with her, tried to jump in until Sa'nai appeared out of nowhere and jumped on one of their backs.

"Y'all thought you were about to jump my motherfucking friend!"

Wham!

Sa'nai punched the girl in the back of the head. The other chick tried to pull her off her and lost focus on Chrissy. My hand rose and I was ready to bash that motherfucker's head in until I was picked up from behind.

"Let me go!" I screamed at the top of my lungs, wiggling in their arms.

"Calm down, Sapphire."

Two muscular men stormed into the section. The guy that Sa'nai was talking to, held Chrissy back, so she couldn't sneak me again. He handed her over to one of the security officers while the other pulled Sa'nai away from the other chicks.

Gripping both of them, he carried them out of the section.

"Your ass going to pay for this shit!" Chrissy screamed as they carried them away. If that bitch even attempted to come my way again, I was going to beat the brakes off her ass.

Kon placed me down on my feet. I was pissed, angry, and all I wanted to do was get the fuck out of there. That bitch had me looking like only God knows what after she snatched my shit off my head.

"You good?" Kon questioned me while his friend checked on Sa'nai.

"Does it fucking look like it?" I snatched my closure up off the floor and stormed off.

"Sapphire!" He caught me by the wrist, stopping me. "I'm sorry about what happened. If you let me, I promise to make it up to you."

I chewed on the inside of my jaw, debating on what I wanted to say. I liked Kon, but if being with him was going to be a circus every day of the fucking week, then I´d pass. No man was worth that much trouble. I had a fucking brand to protect and I wasn't going to let him or anyone else tarnish my shit.

"Nothing like that will happen again. You have my word," he said when he noticed my hesitation.

"You better hope not because I'm gon' beat that bitch black and fucking blue." I crossed my arms over my chest, shifting all my weight to my right side.

Smirking, he hooked my chin and pecked me on the corner of my mouth. "You need me to get you home?"

"Sa'nai and I were going to just catch an Uber."

"Looks like she's well taken care of to me."

My eyes darted in her direction and she was snuggled up with the guy on the couch with a huge smile on her face. I trekked over to where they sat and leaned down by her ear.

"I'ma let Kon take me home. Are you going to be okay?"

"Yeah, I'm good."

"You sure?"

"Sapphire, go home." She laughed, turning her attention back to him.

"I guess you can take me home," I told Kon, sauntering to the exit. The sooner I got out of there the better.

Sa'nai

The next morning...

I stirred in the bed and turned over onto my side, eyes fluttered open, lifting my hand to shield from the light beaming through the window. I instantly knew that I couldn't be in my own bedroom because I had black-out curtains for those purposes.

Easing up in the bed, my eyes roamed around the room to get a feel of where I may have been. I noticed men cologne sitting on the dresser and the clothes lying on the floor.

Is that my—

Glancing down, I realized I was naked. I quickly gripped the sheets, covering my breasts with them and I noted the body lying next to me. I poked him in the back, so I could see who it was. Fucking around with Sapphire, I was drunk as fuck the night before and couldn't really remember most of the shit that happened. I was going to kick Sapphire's ass for even allowing some shit like this to fucking happen.

"Hey!" I shoved him hard in the back.

"What the fuck!" he barked, and goosebumps coursed over my body.

"No!" I bolted from the bed, holding the sheet tightly against my frame. I remembered that voice. It was one that I'd never be able to forget. "What the fuck am I doing here!"

"Why the hell are you screaming and shit?" Blessed finally faced me and I saw he didn't have on a shirt.

"Did we have sex last night?"

"Why you tripping and shit?" Sitting on the edge of the bed, he scratched his head and rose to his feet. "I think I like you better with liquor in your system."

I admired his ass as he strolled into the bathroom. Jumping back on the bed, I spread my legs as far as they would go and touched my pussy to see if Blessed had been anywhere near it. I knew it was possible we could have been naked, but that didn't mean we had to have fucked.

"What the hell are you doing?" he asked, shoving his toothbrush into his mouth.

"You just take advantage of vulnerable people?"

"You were the one that was all over me all got damn night. If you look at it from my point, you wanted the shit. I'on rape people, Ms. Gates or should I say Sa'nai?" He smirked with toothpaste all over his mouth.

The only thing I remembered from the night before was when we first got into the section and I saw Blessed sitting there. It was cool and all being around him, but I didn't think I had gotten that wasted where I slept with him. This was the first time I've ever done anything like that before. Usually, I was more careful.

Snatching my clothes up from the floor, I hurriedly put them on.

"You don't want any breakfast or anything?" He poked his head out the door.

"Do I fucking look like I want some got damn breakfast?" I mugged him.

"So, you just gon' get the dick and dip on a nigga like that?

I feel so fucking used."

I shot him an evil glare. It irritated me how he knew what happened last night and I couldn't remember shit. I really hoped I wasn't bad in bed. My face flushed. I needed to get the hell out of there as fast as possible.

The shower started and his head poked out the bathroom again. I brushed my hair up into a messy ponytail and grabbed my clutch off the floor. Searching inside, I found my phone and it was damn near dead.

"You didn't want to join me in the shower?"

"Does it fucking look like it?" I rushed out of his bedroom and followed the hallway down to the front door.

"Am I going to see you again?" He asked, strolling down the hallway behind me.

"Don't hold your breath."

I slammed the door behind me and exhaled. Blessed wasn't my type of man. I had a nice time talking to him the night before at the club, but I didn't think he'd ever be the type that I'd fall for. I was beyond embarrassed to know that we slept together. Now, the shit was going to drive me completely insane, not knowing what happened or if I was trash.

I hurried out of the building and stopped when I realized that I didn't drive there. Sapphire and I took an Uber to the club, so I was completely carless. Pulling my phone out, I ordered an Uber and posted up against the building, waiting for it to arrive. People eyed me as I walked by, giving me nasty looks and shit. I was doing the walk of shame, leaving that building in my club attire.

The Uber pulled up to the curb and I hopped inside the car. I sat there with my head resting against the seat, thinking about how I was going to push this situation to the back of my mind and forget about the shit.

∞∞∞

Later that day...

The entire day, I kept thinking about what happened the night before and it was driving me completely insane. Getting up from the bed, I grabbed my purse and phone and slipped my feet into my sneakers. Since I didn't want anything to do with Blessed, I decided I was going to go by Sapphire's house and see if she knew what the fuck was going on.

Hopping into my car, I pulled out of the parking deck and went straight to Sapphire's house. When I pulled up, her car was sitting in the driveway, so I knew she was there. Climbing out of the car, I used my key and let myself into the house. It was quiet, so she was probably in there sleeping. If she hadn't been out so late the night before, she wouldn't be sleeping her got damn day away.

Treading down the hallway to her bedroom, I stopped in the doorway and she was sitting Indian style in her bedroom with her MacBook.

"I really think I'ma take my key away from your ass," she said, without even looking up at me. She was too busy typing something on her computer.

Easing on into the room, I gently sat down at the foot of her bed. She cut her eyes at me and I waited until she was done doing whatever she was doing on the computer, so I could go in on her ass for allowing me to fucking leave the club with Blessed.

"What brought you by anyway?" She glanced down at her phone and shut her laptop.

"I didn't wake up in my bed this morning."

She gasped, placing her hand over her chest and eyed me.

"Why the hell did you let me go home with Blessed!" The expression she gave me when I told her that I didn't wake up in my own bed this morning, let me know that she already knew what was going to happen. I needed to fucking understand why she didn't go by our rules and made sure I made it home safe after the club.

"You really call yourself mad with me, right now?"

"You were supposed to make sure that I got home last night, not end up in the bed with that nigga! We had sex, Sapphire!"

I bolted to my feet and paced the floor.

"And what's wrong with that?"

"It was Blessed!"

"You didn't seem too upset about it last night. You were all over that nigga for most of the damn night. I told you I was leaving, and you said that you were good. I asked if you were sure and you said yeah, so don't try and blame that shit on me."

She rose to her feet, grabbing her laptop and left out of the room. I followed down the hallway behind her and she slipped her laptop onto the coffee table and went into her open floor planned kitchen.

"I don't remember anything from last night after going into the section. I woke up this morning naked as the day I was fucking born and him too. I'm not even sure if we had sex or not, and if we did, if I was good or trash. I'd never be able to show my face around him again."

"Why didn't you just ask him if y'all had sex or not?"

I cocked my head to the side. I know damn well she didn't just ask me that dumbass question. We both were naked. Of course, we had sex.

"Really Sapphire?"

She grabbed a bottle of water out of the fridge and went over to the couch.

"I'm not understanding what you want from me, right now." She cut her eyes at me, and I sighed, flopping down on the sofa alongside her.

"Tell me about your night since mine was shit."

"I woke up in my own bed if that's what you mean."

"So, you trying to be fucking funny now."

"I and Kon didn't do anything after we left y'all at the club. He brought me straight home, we did a little bit of talking and he left. But we did have sex at the club."

"Sapphire!"

"What? I was horny as fuck." She rubbed her hand across her hair that was slicked back into a ponytail. She no longer had her sew-in in.

"What happened to your hair?"

"You really don't remember what happened last night?" She turned on the couch, giving me her undivided attention.

"No."

"I got into it with Kon's ex last night. We were fighting, and so were you. You took on two bitches at once."

"You're lying."

"Have I ever lied to you before?"

"That bitch snatched your hair out?"

"Just the closure, so I took all of it down. I'll call Gabby later and schedule an appointment. I had to spend the day canceling shit because Kon doesn't want to have the party anyone. I'm kind of upset because that would have been one of my largest parties ever. I was really looking forward to it." Her head lowered and she scratched behind her ear.

"More parties will come down the line. Don't stress about it." Placing my hand on her thigh, I gently squeezed it.

"I know."

"What do you have planned for the rest of the day?" I shifted on the couch, getting comfortable. It was the weekend, so I didn't really have anything to do. If she wasn't busy, I just might spend my day over there.

"I don't know. You have anything in mind?"

"Not really. Maybe we could order some food or something and watch a few movies."

"Sounds good to me."

Kon

The shit Chrissy did the night before at my club was fucking unacceptable. I don't know what was going through her mind when she showed up there acting a fucking fool. If I had known she was going to act like that, I would have taken her fucking name off the guest list. She knew that I didn't play when it came to putting our business out there in the fucking streets like that and that was the second time she decided she wanted to act a fucking fool in one day.

I had been trying to figure out exactly how I was going to handle the fucking situation with her. Whenever she didn't get her way, she threw temper tantrums and last night was a result of me ending things.

She needed to know that none of this shit was fucking okay. I hated whenever I had to sit her down like a got damn child and talk to her as if I was her father. Maybe her not having a father figure in her life growing up was affecting her as a fucking adult or something.

I understand that she was angry about not being with me anymore, but obviously, she wasn't thinking fucking clearly. If she took money out of my pocket, then that meant taking it out of her own got damn pocket. Everything I did, I did for my daughter to ensure she was going to be straight in the future. Stormie was the reason why I grinded so fucking hard in the got damn streets.

Climbing out of my car, I made my way to the front door

of the house. Since we broke up, I gathered my shit and had been staying in a hotel suite until I could find somewhere I liked, to stay. It was only right that I left Stormie and Chrissy in the house. After all, they were the reasons why I bought the mother-fucker in the first place.

Using my key, I let myself inside.

"Chrissy!" I barked to get a location on her ass.

"What the fuck are you doing here?" She strolled down the steps in a pair of shorts and a t-shirt like she had been loun-ging around all day. "You no longer stay here, so why are you using your key to get in?"

"But I pay the bills in this motherfucker." She rolled her eyes and walked off. I followed closely behind her because I wasn't done with the fucking conversation. "What was that bullshit you pulled last night?"

"Don't tell me you came all the way over here because you're mad that I beat your little hoe's ass last night." She snickered, and I was going to let her keep telling herself that. She caught Sapphire off guard and snatched her hair off, I wouldn't call that beating her ass. If we hadn't separated them when we had, she probably would have made a trip to the hos-pital. Sapphire was about to fuck her ass up with that got damn bottle.

I knew that Sapphire was a little fireball from the way she talked to people who were her clients. She didn't give two fucks when it came to disrespect, but I definitely wasn't expecting her to try and beat Chrissy's ass with a bottle.

"You were in the fucking wrong and you fucking know it."

Spinning on her heels, she faced me with wide eyes. "I was in the wrong!" she shouted, poking herself in the chest.

"You were in there acting a got damn fool like you aren't taking money and food out your own child's mouth. The money

I make from that club goes to you and her and you fucking know it. The least you could do is walk around here like you got fucking sense."

Boom!

She slammed her hand down on the marble island in the kitchen and her eyes damn near popped from her fucking head. "You fucking disrespected me! You lied to my motherfucking face that you weren't fucking cheating on me, but I caught you and her ass at the club last night!"

"That wasn't cheating. We were no longer together when I met up with her."

"So, you left me to be with her?"

"No. You know damn well why I left your ass. It's how you're fucking acting now."

"I still don't believe a motherfucking thing you say. You were fucking that bitch and that's why you left and that's exactly what the fuck I'ma tell everyone."

"See, that's your got damn problem now. You run your fucking mouth too fucking mouth. How is it their got damn business knowing why we broke up in the first place?"

"I'ma let everybody know how you fucking treated me, Kon!"

"Daddy?" Turning on my heels, I saw Stormie standing in the doorway. She was the spitting image of me with her mother's hair. If it wasn't for that little girl, I don't think I would have put up with Chrissy for as long as I had.

"Hey, baby girl." Leaning down, I scooped her up into my arms, pecking her on the cheek.

"When are you coming back home?"

I could feel Chrissy burning a hole in the back of my head. I hated to have to leave my daughter behind the way I had, but I had no other choice. Her mother and I weren't working out, and I wasn't about to risk my happiness any longer trying to force shit to work.

"Mommy and I need a break from each other." That was the best way I could put it at the moment.

"But why?"

"Yeah, why Kon?" Chrissy appeared at my side being messy as hell when all she had to do was shut her fucking mouth.

"We just need a break."

Pecking her on the forehead, I set her down on her feet.

"I have to get going," I told them, treading toward the front door. I would have taken Stormie with me if I was going back to the hotel to spend a little time with her, but I wasn't going in that direction just yet. I wanted to go by and check on Sapphire. She told me that she was alright the night before. She seemed alright when I left her, but I just wanted to stop by to make sure.

"You can't even spend time with your daughter!" Chrissy stormed behind me. She was trying her best to make me out to be the bad person. Everyone that knew me, knew that I spent as much time with Stormie as possible. I didn't want her growing up not knowing her father and turn out like her mother. Sometimes I was too busy to do the things I should, and would ask Blessed to take my place, but I made damn sure to make up for the shit later down the line.

"Why you always with the bullshit, Chrissy?" Halting my steps, she crashed into my back. "I moved out yesterday and you talking like I've been gone a got damn month or something and hadn't seen my damn daughter. You gon' stop trying to make me seem like less of a fucking father when you know damn well, I give her and your ass the motherfucking world."

"But you cheated on me, though!" She shoved me hard in the chest and I just ignored the shit. She was angry, so I let it slide.

"I'm not going there with you anymore." Spinning on my heels, I left out of the house.

"I promise you gon' regret leaving me!" she shouted behind me and slammed the front door.

Shaking my head, I climbed into my car and sat there for a moment. I didn't even feel bad about breaking up with Chrissy. All the bullshit she was doing just proved that I made the right choice ending shit when I did. She was toxic as fuck and I didn't need that shit in my life.

Collecting my thoughts, I placed the car in drive and pulled out of the driveway. It took me almost forty-five minutes to make it to Sapphire's house. I wasn't sure if she was at home or her office, but I was trying her house first since it was the closest.

Pulling up in front of it, I saw her car sitting in the driveway, so I got out and neared the door.

Knock! Knock!

It took her a couple of minutes, but she finally came to it. When her eyes landed on me, a smile crept on her face. I didn't think she was going to be excited to see me after the shit that happened the night before which was sort of my fault.

"What are you doing here?" She stepped to the side, allowing me access to her home.

"Wanted to come by and check on you, if that's alright with you."

"Guess so."

Shutting the door behind me, she walked over to the couch, plopping down with one of her legs, resting underneath her.

"I see you took your hair down."

"Yup." She brushed her hand across her slicked-back hair. Sapphire was far from ball-headed, so I didn't understand how come she wore all that weave in the first place.

"I'm really sorry about what happened last night." I took a seat on the couch alongside her and immediately, her scent crept up my nostrils. Every time I was near Sapphire, she smelled good as fuck and it made it hard for me to resist her. Even now, she was dressed down in a pair of black tights and a white t-shirt, smelling like she was fresh out the got damn shower.

"You don't have to keep apologizing for something she did. Like I told you last night, it wasn't your fault."

"I know... but I still feel like it is."

She stared into my eyes and her face flushed. Quickly turning away, she took her attention to her cell phone.

"I enjoyed spending time with you last night. For the first time, I didn't have to worry about shit ending in an argument."

"But it did." She snickered, pertaining to the fight she ended up in with Chrissy.

"You know what I meant."

"I know. I had fun too." Her glistening eyes met mine again.

"I want to take you on a real date."

"Really?" Her eyes lit up when I said that. I wasn't sure if it was because she hadn't been on one in a while or the fact that she probably thought I just wanted pussy from her. That wasn't my motive. I wasn't the type of guy to go around sleeping with random ass women especially without a condom. I liked Sapphire and just wanted to get to know her a little bit better. Some might think it was a little too early for that shit, but time was valuable to me and I hated to waste the motherfucker. "Yeah, is that a problem?"

"No." She smiled from ear to ear. "Where are you talking about taking me?"

"Let me worry about all that."

I know she was used to being in control and shit, but it was my idea to take her on a date, so I was going to do my best to plan the perfect night for her. Chrissy and I had become comfortable as fuck. It seemed like forever since we last went on a date somewhere. Maybe that was our problem. We had become content with each other and gave up on the relationship.

"Can I at least get a hint?"

"Nope." I smirked, rising to my feet and she quickly shot to mine.

"How else am I supposed to know what to wear?"

"I'ma handle all that shit. I have to get out of here though. I'll hit you up later."

Cupping her face, I pecked her gently on her soft lips and left out of there.

Blessed

A couple of days later...

Ever since Sa'nai walked out on me, she had been the only thing on my fucking mind and the shit was crazy. I had never come across a girl that could keep my focus like that. Most of the time, I fucked and was done with their ass, but not Sa'nai.

Even though we had drunk ass sex, I still remembered every single thing that happened that night. She had some of the best pussy I'd ever come across. I thought about trying to reach out to her, but I didn't have her phone number. The way she ran out of there that morning, I was pretty sure she didn't want anything else to do with my ass.

"Blessed!" Kon barked, bringing me back from my thoughts.

I gazed over at him and a mug rested on his face with a blunt dangling from his lips. He was talking about some irrelevant ass shit when I stepped into his office and my mind drifted elsewhere.

"Did you hear what I said?"

"No."

"You really need to pay fucking attention. You think this shit a fucking game?" He took a puff from the blunt, dumped the ashes in the ashtray and handed it over to me.

"What the hell are you talking about?"

"It's some new nigga in town. He thinks he gon' take over our territory."

"That's a motherfucking lie. Who the fuck is the nigga?"

"I'on know. He calls himself Thugga or some shit."

"You don't know where he at? We can go end that shit right fucking now if you want to." I pulled my strap from my waistline and slammed it down on the desk.

"Hell no. I don't even know what the motherfucker looks like, but what I do know is that we need to get his ass out the fucking picture."

"I'll put my ear to the streets and see what I can find out about this nigga." Glancing down at my phone, I noticed the time. "I gotta get outta here. I'll fuck with you later." Taking one last drag from the blunt, I handed it back over to him.

"Where the hell are you going in such a hurry?"

"To take care of some business." A smile passed my lips as I headed out of his office and out the side exit to the warehouse.

Hitting the fob, I climbed into my car and pulled off. It was almost time for school to get out and I wanted to pop up on Sa'nai since I knew no other way to get in contact with her. I wasn't sure how she was going to react when she saw me, but hopefully, it would be better than the last time.

Pulling up to the building, I tossed my truck in park and watched as all the children hopped on the buses and got into their parents' cars. I didn't see Sa'nai anywhere, but I knew she'd turn up soon to get ready to go home.

I sat out there in that parking lot for thirty minutes waiting for her to come out the door. For a moment, I thought that maybe she wasn't there, and I'd just have to try and catch her another time until I saw her exit the building. She wore this black pants suit with a red blouse underneath. Her hair was pulled back into a ball at the nape of her neck. She strutted down those steps as if she was on a fucking runway. She damn sure looked like she belonged on one.

Swiftly hopping from my truck, I rushed across the parking lot where I saw her heading to her car. "Sa'nai!" I called out her name, and she stopped in her tracks.

Facing me, she asked, "What are you doing here?"

"I wanted to see you again." I strolled closer to her and her beauty almost took my breath away. She gazed at me with her dark eyes. From her facial expression, I knew she wasn't happy to see me.

"Why?" Jingling her keys in her hands, she turned and sped walked toward her red Audi.

"I'm sorry about the other night," I said in hopes that that would help me. It wasn't my fault that she couldn't hold her fucking liquor and kept throwing herself at me. I know I shouldn't have had sex with her while she was vulnerable, but shit, I was too. She wasn't the only motherfucker that was drunk as fuck. I was so over my fucking limit that I had to order a got damn Uber to get home. I never used public transportation because I had trust issues and didn't know who the hell was out to get me. If she wasn't with me, I would have taken my chances of driving myself home.

"That doesn't fix what happened."

"I know, but we both were fucked up and something happened between us that I think we had been wanting to happen since the first day we met." Nearing her, I pinned her against her car. Her eyes bore into mine.

"How was it?" Her teeth sank into her lower lip and I knew I was telling the truth. I gave her ass exactly what she wanted.

"For someone that's mad about what happened, you

wanna know how the pussy was?" Cupping her chin, I licked my lips and her body shifted.

"Can you just answer the fucking question. The shit has been driving me fucking crazy." She snatched away from me. My fingertips grazed her arms and goosebumps coursed over her skin.

"Why don't I just show you instead of tell you?"

"No—" I silenced her with my lips. My hands slid up her stomach, groping her breasts and she moaned against my lips.

"Will you stop talking and just give in?"

Her arms draped around my neck and her lips crashed against mine again. I wanted Sa'nai again. I wanted to feel her while I was sober. I wanted to see how wet that pussy could get for me while she was sober.

Peeling away from me, she said, "Follow me home."

I didn't even wait for her to change her mind. I hurried up to my truck, so she wouldn't leave me. Hopping into my truck, I pulled out of the parking lot behind her. It didn't take us long to make it to her apartment. Parking directly next to her car, I hopped out and she quickly gripped my hand, leading me into the building.

My heart pounded in my chest as she stuck her key into the hole to open the door. That shit had never happened to me before. I was hoping that once she and I had sex again, I'd be able to forget all about her and move on. Hopefully, that shit didn't mean I was going to end up being crazy over her ass like most niggas I see out in the streets and be making fun of. Those niggas be so got damn pussy-whipped that it was a fucking shame. Some of them would cut a bitch's grass with eyebrow scissors.

The door pushed open and she yanked me into the apartment and kicked her shoes off at the door. Our lips meshed, and I pushed her jacket back off her shoulders. Unbuttoning her blouse, she pulled it off, tossing it to the floor. I gazed at her breasts trapped behind the black laced bra.

Cupping her face, I locked our lips again and scooped her up into my arms by the ass. I wasn't sure where her bedroom was, but after a few bumps and laughs, I finally found it. Gently laying her down on the bed, I straightened my posture and pulled my shirt over my head, tossing it to the floor. Her eyes embraced my frame and from the lust oozing from them, I could tell she liked what she saw.

Unclasping her bra, she slung it across the room and hurriedly pulled her pants and panties down. Sa'nai wasn't playing any games about getting the dick, so I knew I was going to have to bring it. I pushed my pants and boxer briefs down and she gripped me by the waist, pulling me closer to her.

Licking her lips, she stuffed my dick into her mouth. Her tongue brushed against it and my eyes rolled to the back of my head. She sucked my dick better than any other bitch had before. Sa'nai was sucking licking and slurping the hell out of my shit.

The tip of my head repeatedly tapped at the back of her throat. My toes curled, popping in my socks. My climax washed over my body and my seeds released down her throat. She swallowed it all and sat back on her knees, sticking her tongue out to let me know that it was all gone.

That shit was sexy as fuck to me whenever a female would swallow semen. Most of them got in their fucking feelings whenever they were asked to do some shit like that. The way she just did it without me having to ask her to. She just might be a keeper.

Climbing onto the bed, I cupped her by the face and shoved my tongue down her throat. She gently laid back onto her back and I pushed her legs apart with my knee, hovering over her. I positioned my dick at her opening and gazed down into her face to make sure that was really what she wanted.

"What are you waiting for?"

Slowly entering her, her eyes rolled to the back of her head and her teeth sank into her lower lip. Her pussy was slippery and tight, just the way I liked it. My pace picked up and she dug her nails into my back.

"You like that shit?" I asked her, planting kisses on the side of her neck.

"Shut up and just fuck me," she moaned.

I wrapped my hand around her throat and lightly squeezed. Her legs opened up even further, giving me more access to her pussy.

"Fuck, right there."

I held my pace and tapped her g-spot repeatedly. Her legs trembled and I knew she was close to climaxing. I was trying my best to hold my nut until she released. The last thing I wanted to do was leave her unsatisfied.

Her grip grew tighter on me and I felt her juices gush.

"Fuuuuck!" she cried out and I finally released my seeds inside her and pulled out, dropping alongside her.

"I wasn't missing anything." She popped up in bed and tread toward the bathroom.

"Are you fucking serious?" I sat up, gazing into the bathroom. She leaned over into the walk-in shower and turned it on.

"Yeah, I actually thought I missed something while I was drunk."

This motherfucker had to be fucking kidding me. Shooting from the bed, I hurried into the bathroom behind her. She stumbled back against the sink as I neared her. Her eyes peered up into mine.

"Why I think you're lying."

"But I'm not."

"Let me fix this shit then." Scooping her up into my arms, I carried her into the shower. We went for another round and she came at least six times before we got cleaned up and exited the shower. All that shit she was talking, but she was in there screaming my fucking name at the top of her lungs. If I didn't know any better, I felt like she did that shit because she wanted another round.

"If you wanted to go another round, then you could have just said that," I told her, slipping my shirt over my head.

"I don't know what you're talking about." She rummaged through her drawers looking for something to put on.

"That's what your mouth says."

I finished getting dressed and she stood there in a large t-shirt and some panties. She tugged on the bottom of it when she noticed me eyeing her.

"You know where the door is. I'm about to take me a nap." She hurried over to the bed and pulled the dirty sheets off, tossing them to the floor. I felt like one of the hoes I threw out of my house after we were done fucking.

"You just gon' throw a nigga out like that?"

"Goodbye Blessed," she said, not even glancing in my direction. Without saying another word, I trekked toward the front door.

Sapphire

A couple of days later...

"**A**nd you absolutely sure that the flowers are going to get in on time?" I asked Tabitha through the phone. I had another wedding coming up in a few days and I planned on that one going better than the one before. Sherry's wedding still fucked with me a little bit. I hated that I took away from her having her happy ending, but at least she didn't end up marrying a frog.

"I promise it'll be here."

A knock on my office door grasped my attention. I glanced in that direction and Sasha poked her head inside. I beckoned for her to enter, knowing that my call was about to come to an end.

"It better be, and they better be the ones I asked for I'll call back in a couple of days to make sure they arrived."

"Okay."

Ending the call, I slid my phone onto my desk and released a sigh.

"These came for you," Sasha said, setting the flowers down on the desk. They were beautiful as hell—pink and blue tinted roses.

"Who sent them?" I asked her and she shrugged.

"There's a card in there. You know I wasn't going to go through your things."

Taking a whiff of the flowers, I pulled the card out and read it.

Can't wait to see you tonight. Everything you'll need is at home. -Kon

I couldn't stop the huge smile that spread across my face. I had been talking to Kon every single day. He'd text me in the mornings and before he goes to bed, but he hadn't said anything about our date. When he first brought that shit up, I thought he was just talking. He didn't look like the type that would go on dates like that. I wasn't even sure if I wanted to get attached to him like that. He did just come out of a relationship and the last thing I wanted was to get hurt by some nigga just because he decided he wanted to go back to his baby mother.

"Thank you," I told Sasha, letting her know that she could leave.

Soon as the door shut, I grabbed my personal phone and dialed Kon's number with the widest, dumbest smile on my face.

"I take it you got my flowers." He answered.

"They're beautiful." I gushed.

"Just like you."

"How come you didn't tell me that you were trying to take me out tonight?"

"I told you I had everything under control."

"But how you know I didn't have any plans."

"Because Sasha looked at your calendar for me."

"Remind me to fire her."

"You can't fire that girl for doing her fucking job."

"Going through my shit isn't in her job description."

"She didn't want to do it, I had to do a little bit of persuading."

"So, are you going to tell me where we're going or what?"

"Just be ready by eight."

The call ended and I stared at the phone in awe. I couldn't believe that nigga had the fucking audacity to hang the phone up in my face.

"Sasha!" I called out her name and she poked her head in the door. She knew she was in fucking trouble because she didn't want to come all the way into the office.

"Ma'am?"

"Don't fucking ma'am me. You're lucky that I like Kon or else your little ass would be fired," I said, rising from my chair. It was going on four and I knew if I wanted to be ready on time, I needed to get my ass home and dressed.

"I'm sorry, but he didn't really give me much of a choice."

"Uh huh, you're off the hook this time."

I swiftly gathered my things and hurried toward the door. "Next time someone tells you to go through my things, say something to me about it."

She rushed behind me toward the elevator. "I think its sweet that he wanted to surprise you like that."

"Let me guess... you were his way of getting into my house too."

Sasha and Sa'nai were the only ones that had a key to my house. The only reason Sasha had one was because she was my assistant, and sometimes I worked from home. There were several tasks I had her do that included making a trip to my home office and picking up certain things when I had a tendency to leave them.

"Just wait until you see what he left there. You'll be thanking me."

"You better hope so." The elevator doors shut on me and I checked the time on my phone to see exactly how much I had left to get ready for my date. It seemed like forever since I was last on one, and I couldn't wait to see what Kon had planned for me.

When I arrived home, I dropped my belongings on the chair in the living room and went straight to my bedroom to see what was in there. Lying on my bed was this silk gray dress and silver diamond Christian Louboutin heels. The dress was simple as hell, but I was sure once I slipped it on, it was going to pop.

Smiling, I pulled my hair up and wrapped it with my silk scarf and headed into the bathroom. The water was already ran for me. I stuck my index finger down into it and it was still hot which only meant when I was talking to Kon, he was probably still at my fucking house.

Sitting on the edge of the tub was a bottle of Stella Black and a glass. I didn't know how he knew that was one of my favorite wines.

"Sasha." I laughed to myself and stripped out of my clothes.

Climbing over into the tub, I rested against the base of the tub and a moan escaped my lips. The hot water felt good against my body. I had been on my feet ever since six that morning and now I had a chance to relax for a little while.

Pouring myself a glass of wine, I took a sip from it and my mind drifted off to Kon. I couldn't wait to land my eyes on that man when he got here. From the way he had me feeling that night in the club, he'd be lucky if I let him leave the house at all.

Christina "Chrissy" Wallace

A couple of days later...

My mind had been fucked up ever since Kon brought his ass to the fucking house and called himself trying to got damn check me. I should have been checking his ass for the way he was handling me and shit, treating me like some random bitch.

How the fuck did he think I was going to react when I found out that he had fucking broke up with me to be with that bitch. I knew something wasn't right when I saw them smiling and shit in each other's face through that window of that bakery. Shit looked like a fucking date to me, and that's the reason why I just couldn't drop the shit once we made it home. Something wasn't adding up and that shit was confirmed when I saw them snuggled up in his section at the got damn club like he hadn't just broken up with me.

What angered me even more was the fact of how he was moving on so got damn fast. It was as if that was his fucking plan all along and he was just waiting for the moment where he could get a clean break. That motherfucker was going to regret leaving me in the fucking dust like everything was okay. I don't give a damn if he let me keep that stupid ass house and cars. I fucking earned that shit after putting nine years in with his bitch ass.

Slipping into this brown Fendi tube dress, I eased my feet into my Fendi slides and glanced down at the time. It was almost time for me to meet Serenity for lunch at this new restaurant called *Crab Nation.* She had been trying to get me out of the house for the last few days, but with me having Stormie at home, I couldn't really go anywhere. This morning, Kon had come and picked her up for a couple of days. The motherfucker didn't even bother to get out of the car or anything. He just pulled into the driveway and called her phone, letting her know he was outside. I wouldn't have known she was gone if she hadn't come in there to say goodbye.

Hurrying, I removed my scarf from my head and ran my detangling brush through my hair. After taking a glance in my floor-length mirror, I was out the door.

Pulling up to the restaurant, I jumped out of the car and passed valet the keys. I wasn't sure what type of restaurant this was with valet and shit for some crabs, but I couldn't wait to find out what it looked like on the inside.

Every new business that touched Miami, Serenity dragged me out to give it a try. She loved trying shit, but sometimes, it didn't work out in her favor. When she brought up the idea of coming here, I thought what harm could it do? I love crabs and wouldn't mind giving them a try. They just might end up being my new favorite place.

Entering the building, I was stopped by the hostess standing behind the booth. "How many?" she questioned, gathering the menus.

"I'm meeting a friend here. She should already be here," I told her, eyes skimming the building. Serenity was huge on being on time. I was five minutes later, so I knew she was already there somewhere. When my eyes landed on her sitting at a table by the far window, a smile crept on my face. "I see her."

Walking toward Serenity, she rose to her feet to greet me.

"I should have known your ass was going to be late." She pecked me on the cheek and sat back down.

"Just five minutes, Serenity." Shaking my head, I sat down in front of her.

"I'm surprised it was just that."

"Whatever." I sighed, grabbing the menu going straight to the drinks section. "What do they have good to drink?" I quizzed her, scanning the menu.

"You sound tensed."

"I am."

"Don't tell me it's Kon again." I noted the distaste in her voice. Ever since Kon and I first got together, she never liked him, and I didn't really understand why. She wanted me to be with someone else, but my life with Kon was great up until the point I got to thinking he was cheating on me. It's not like the thoughts just magically jumped into my mind. We went from having sex twice a day to not having the shit at all. He'd go months without touching me in that way. Of course, I was going to get to thinking that someone else was in the fucking picture.

"You know it." I waved my hand in the air to order me something to drink. If we were about to have this conversation, I damn sure couldn't do it sober.

"I don't know why you got with that nigga in the first place. There were so many men after you, but you chose a nigga that sells fucking drugs. How long did you think the shit between you two was going to last? It's what those type of niggas do, Chrissy. They see the next best thing and go for the shit. It doesn't matter how long you've been there. You're old to him now. He wants something new, so he kicked you to the curb for it." She shrugged her shoulders and glanced down at her vibrating phone.

My hand waved in the air a little bit harder to try and gain the waiter's attention. I didn't have a comeback for what Serenity said. She tried her best to talk me out of dating Kon, but I just wouldn't listen. Now, look at me... I'm on the outside looking in after giving this nigga almost a fucking decade of my got damn life.

"What can I get for you?" the waiter asked when he finally found his way over to our table. I thought I was going to have to get up and go find one.

"Let me get a long island iced tea and keep them coming." Nodding, he left the table. "I'm not saying that you're wrong, Serenity, but I love Kon. He broke my heart and there's nothing I can do about it."

"What if there is?" this masculine voice asked from behind me. I hadn't realized we were sitting so fucking close to the other tables and other people could be deep in our conversation. Had I known that, I would have waited until we left to go into detail with her about my failing relationship.

A guy stepped to our table and he was sexy as hell. He was tall, towering over us, probably standing about a good six-three. His skin was dark and smooth, and he had this beard that lined his face. From the shape of it, I could tell he took damn good care of his facial hair. The way he was dressed in that tailored navy-blue suit, I figured he might have been a lawyer or something.

"You were listening to our conversation?" I finally spoke, breaking the trance he had me trapped in.

"I'm sorry, but when you said the name Kon, I couldn't help but to eavesdrop." He licked his plump lips and grabbed the chair from his table, making himself comfortable at ours. My eyes locked with Serenity and her brow rose. All she saw was a good-looking man and probably wouldn't mind climbing that tree. Maybe that's exactly what I needed—to get me some dick and my mind would clear of all the anger I had toward Kon.

"You know my baby daddy?"

"Not personally, but I think we have a common factor here."

"And what is that?" The waiter placed my drink down on the table in front of me and I took a sip from it. I was anxious to see exactly what he had to say.

"Kon... you're pissed with him for cheating on you and leaving you. You want to get him back for hurting you and I'm just the guy to help you do it."

"Oh really? And why do you want to help me?"

Serenity leaned over onto the table, giving the mystery guy her undivided attention. I'm sure she was all for getting Kon back for hurting me.

"I'm new in town and that nigga got something I want."

"What's that?"

"The title of being the King of Miami."

"You're not serious?" Serenity questioned him and burst out laughing. "Is he serious?" She glanced in my direction. I didn't know this man from a can of paint, so how the hell was I supposed to know when he was joking or being serious.

"I'm very much serious." He turned his attention back to me. "If you help me out, then I can help you, and we both win."

"I don't know what you expect me to do."

"Give me all the information that you have on Kon and I'll do everything else."

Serenity swiftly reached across the table and caught me by the arm. "If you do that and Kon finds out... he'll fucking kill you and you know it."

I stared at her for a moment, debating on what I was going to say. She was right, for that type of betrayal, Kon would surely place a bullet in my ass, baby mama or not. This man was asking me to do something dangerous that could put my fucking life in danger. How did I know he wouldn't flip on me and do away with me once he got what he wanted? There was so much to think about in a situation like that.

"I don't know about all that."

"What if I can promise you your safety? He wouldn't even know that you had something to do with it."

I took another sip from my drink and gazed into space. This man was talking a good game. Hurting Kon as much as he hurt me was definitely something I wanted to do. If he took everything away from him and broke his ass down, that shit would be priceless. But what's the cost if I got caught in the middle and became collateral damage?

Kon could do a lot of shit to me if he found out I had been planning against him. He could kill me, or take Stormie away from me where I wouldn't be able to see her again, or he could take everything he allowed me to keep and force me to go back home to my mother—the one place I said I'd never go running back to.

"I'm sorry, but I can't help you." I went back to looking at the menu in hopes he'd just get up and leave our table.

After two minutes of silence, I guess he finally got the hint and rose to his feet. Digging into his pocket, he pulled out a card and slid it onto the table directly in front of me. My gaze met his as he licked his lips, scrubbing his hand across his mouth.

"In case you change your mind."

"I won't." I took my eyes back to the menu and he left our table. Whatever business he may have had in that restaurant must was over with because after placing his chair back at the table, he left.

"Can you believe him?" I laughed, pointing my thumb over my shoulder.

"I actually thought that nigga was just talking."

I glanced down at the business card and caught his name—Thugga. The shit he was offering was tempting as fuck, but I had other shit to think about that was more important than taking down Kon. I've thought of some ways I could get him back like busting the windows out of his cars or flattening his tires. I even thought about finding out where that little ho worked, so I could cause damage to her ass as well, but Thugga was trying to take shit to another level.

The remainder of Serenity and my lunch date, we sat there in silence. I know she was still thinking about the shit Thugga had said from the way she kept eyeing me. She probably thought I was going to be stupid enough to fall into his trap.

We finished lunch and went our separate ways. Instead of going home, I went by the YVE Hotel Miami to pick Stormie up. Kon had texted me toward the end of lunch and asked if I could come and pick her up. He was supposed to have her for another day, but I wasn't complaining. It was lonely as fuck being in that big ass house alone.

Pulling up to the hotel room, I got out of the car and entered, going straight for the elevator. I already knew what room he was in and decided to go up and get Stormie instead of calling and telling her to come down. I thought that maybe I'd be able to talk some sense into Kon about coming back home. The only way I was going to be able to do that was if I promised him not to nag him the way I had before.

I knocked on the door and waited for him to come to it. When it pulled open, a smile graced my face. Kon stood there looking handsome as ever with his shirt off and in a pair of dark denim jeans. I'm not sure if I caught him when he was getting out of the shower or what.

"Stormie! Your mama at the door!" he shouted over his shoulder.

"Kon—" His name got caught in my throat. I wasn't sure how he was going to react when I told him this.

"Yeah?" His brow rose as he stared at me.

"I was wondering if we could talk before I take Stormie home."

"Talk about what?"

"Uh... us."

"There's nothing to talk about and you fucking know it, Chrissy."

"Why you have to act that way toward me?"

"You already know what the deal is, Chrissy. Why don't you just move on and leave the shit alone."

"Move on?" I laughed to try and hide the pain. "You mean like you did when you started fucking that bitch behind my back?" Tears filled my eyes and I could no longer hold the shit back.

"Kon, are you ready?" A woman's voice asked, grasping my attention. I swiftly turned around and saw the little hoe standing there.

"I know damn well you didn't call me to get our daughter, so you could run off with this bitch."

"Watch your fucking mouth," Kon seethed. He stepped out into the hallway and grabbed her as if he thought I was going to do something to her ass.

"You know what, I don't give a damn what your ass has planned. Better work Stormie into the shit." Stormie appeared at the door with her book bag draped over her shoulder. "Change of plans, sweetie, you're staying with your father." I pecked her on the center of her forehead and walked off.

Tears coated my face. Kon called out my name, but I kept

trekking for the elevator. He had me fucked up if he thought I was going to take our daughter on the day he was supposed to have her, so he could go out with that bitch. Whatever motherfucking plans he had was fucking canceled.

Exiting the building, I hit the fob on my car and climbed inside. My eyes landed on the card Thugga had left me earlier.

"Fuck it," I said to myself and picked the card up, dialing his number. Soon as he answered the phone, I said, "I'm in." Everything Kon gave a fuck about was about to be snatched the fuck away from him.

Sa'nai

Two weeks later...

I laid there, staring up at the ceiling not even being able to believe that I allowed Blessed to talk me out of my fucking panties for the tenth day. Ever since the first day we had sex, we'd been fucking like jackrabbits every chance we got.

I said I wasn't going to deal with him, but I kept finding myself right back on his dick. There should have been some form of law that stated that this shit was illegal. I don't even remember the last time I was sprung off some dick like that.

All my previous relationships didn't last long. For whatever reason, it was hard for me to keep a nigga. Don't get me wrong, everything was great on my end, but it was them that always seemed to fuck up.

For instance, I was in a relationship with this guy and everything seemed perfect as hell. The wheels in my mind got to rolling and I got to digging, and you know what they always say, when you go looking for something, you find more than what you were looking for. That statement held its ground when I found out that Troy was married with children. I couldn't believe that shit and wished that I hadn't gone looking, then maybe I would have been able to hold on to that fairytale a little while longer.

Blessed's phone rang and he shifted in bed. I turned over onto my side and stared at his tattooed back as he answered his phone. I'm not sure what was said, but he jumped from the bed and grabbed his clothes off the floor, fleeing to the bathroom. I was used to him doing shit like that whenever we were together. I wasn't sure where he was running off to, and it really wasn't my fucking business. That nigga just better not have brought shit to my fucking doorstep or gave me a motherfucking thing, or we were going to have some serious problems.

I lay there in bed, listening to the shower run, knowing he was about to dip on me. I wasn't sweating the shit though, he'd spent the night with me, and that's more than a lot of niggas got out of me lately.

The water shut off and he emerged from the bathroom fully dressed. Sitting up in bed, my gaze briefly met his.

"What do you have planned for the day?"

"I don't know," I answered him, picking at my fingernails. Since it was the weekend, I didn't have to go to work. Sapphire and I had just got our nails and hair done the other day, so that was out of the question as well. "Maybe just lounge around the house for the day."

"Sounds like fun. Wish I could do that shit, but I got some business I need to take care of."

"I'm sure you do."

He grabbed his sneakers and plopped down on the edge of the bed. "The fuck is that supposed to mean?"

"Nothing."

I sprung to my feet and went into the bathroom to brush my teeth.

"Oh, it meant something."

Rolling my eyes, I shoved my toothbrush into my mouth before I said something to him that I might later regret.

"I'll hit you up later when I'm done doing what I'm doing."

He pecked me on the cheek, and I wiped the shit off with my hand. I couldn't believe I was actually getting in my fucking feelings about him leaving. Normally, it didn't matter, and I was ready for him to get the fuck up out of there, but today just felt different.

Soon as Blessed left out of the room, I gagged and threw up in the sink. I thought maybe I had pushed my toothbrush to the back of my tongue too far or something until I felt more vomit seeping up my throat. I rushed over to the toilet and puked up what felt like my fucking insides.

"How did I catch a virus?" I asked myself, flopping back onto my ass, and sat there for a moment to make sure I didn't have to throw up anymore.

I wasn't sure what the hell was wrong with me, but I was going to jump in the shower and make a trip to the grocery store to grab a few things in case the shit decided it wanted to get worse.

Jumping in the shower, I took a quick thirty-minute shower and got out of there. I was nauseous and didn't want to end up vomiting while I was in there.

After getting dressed in a pair of black biker shorts and a black t-shirt, I dialed Sapphire's number on my way out the front door. For someone that worked at a school, you'd think I was used to getting sick by now, but I wasn't. Viruses and more shit hit me during the year if one of the children came to school sick and I didn't know it. I tried my best to keep everything wiped down in the classroom, but there were still times I ended up getting sick.

Sapphire was always my saving grace when it came to being sick. I'm not sure what the fuck it was about her, but she always fucking knew what to do. I told her, that she was going to make the best mother one day whenever she decided to have children. She always laughed the shit off because she didn't think she'd ever have a child with her career, but anything was possible in my book.

"Hey boo," she answered the phone sounding all cheerful and shit. She'd been like that since she been messing around with Kon's ass. If he was making my girl this happy, then I was all for the shit.

"I need some advice."

"If you're calling me about sucking Blessed's dick then I can't help you."

I hated her ass sometimes.

She thought it was funny as fuck when I told her I messed around and slipped on the dick. She told me it was much needed to help me loosen up a little bit, but I didn't think I was fucking tight or anything. I just had been being cautious of who I wanted to deal with.

"It's nothing like that. I woke up not feeling well this morning. You know every time I get sick, I call you for some advice." She was the only person I could call. I didn't have any family with me growing up in the system. My last foster mother was cool and all, but she made sure I got into college, so I could get out of her house the moment I graduated. Sapphire and I had met while we were freshmen in college and have been inseparable ever since.

"What's wrong with you?"

"I've been vomiting. I think I may have caught a bug from one of the children at school. What do you think I should get from the store to help?" I asked her, pulling into Publix's parking lot. Publix was one of my all-time favorite grocery stores. Some people complained about the prices in there, but I loved their quality.

"Um, try getting you some saltine crackers and Ginger Ale, oh, and some soup. Maybe your stomach will settle down soon, but that's the best I can think of right now."

"I sure as hell didn't plan on being stuck in the house today. If I caught a virus, I probably passed it to Blessed too."

"You'll know before the day is over." She laughed, but I didn't find shit funny.

I entered the store and grabbed everything she told me to get. Sapphire was still talking on the phone, rambling about something when I passed the aisle with the feminine products. I backtracked when my eyes landed on the pregnancy tests.

"I couldn't be." I shook my head. But I had been kind of careless with Blessed, so it was a possibility. Even though I loved children—which was one of the reasons why I began teaching in the first place, having them never crossed my mind before. I never came across a guy that I wanted to have one by except for Troy, and he quickly ruined that fantasy for me. In a way, I never wanted to turn into just someone's baby mama.

"What did you say?" Sapphire quizzed me, bringing me from my thoughts.

"Nothing." I eased onto the aisle and my heart thumped rapidly in my chest. "I think I have everything. I'm about to check out. I'll call you back later." I swiftly ended the call before she could say anything else and my eyes trained on the pregnancy tests. Something inside me told me to get one, then the other part of me argued that I didn't need one.

"It won't hurt to find out," I told myself, grabbing the closest test and jetted off the aisle before someone saw me. I was a grown ass woman and was terrified that someone might see me buying a test and my business would be all over the fucking city. Sapphire would fucking kill me if she found out some shit like that from someone else's mouth, and the last thing I wanted to happen was Blessed get a hold of the shit before I even knew what the result was.

I didn't know if he wanted children either. We rarely talked whenever he would come over. It was mostly fucking for us and I liked it that way... at least I thought I did until that little mishap this morning before he left.

Climbing back into the car, I rushed home, so I could take that test, and get rid of the anticipation that was eating me alive. If I didn't do it, it was going to be the only thing I thought about until I got up enough nerves to. Pulling into the parking spot, I hopped from the car and went inside. After dropping my groceries down on the counter in the kitchen, I went straight into the bathroom and opened the box.

Sitting on the toilet, I chewed on my fingernails, feeling my pressure rise as I thought about the results for my test. I hadn't even taken it yet, and I was already scared shitless to see what it was going to say. In my mind, I had a virus, and if God was on my side I was going to walk out of that bathroom still with one.

I peed on the stick and set it down on the sink. My nerves were so fucked up that I didn't even bother to get up afterward. I was going to sit there until those three minutes were up and I saw what my results were.

My phone beeped, letting me know that my three minutes were up. I chewed on the inside of my jaw and grabbed the test. My eyes expanded when I saw the positive.

"This can't be right."

Tossing the stick back onto the counter, I grabbed the other test out of the box and peed on that one as well. My eyes watered as I stared at the positive on that one as well. I brushed my hair back out of my face with my hand and sighed.

Getting up from the toilet, I dialed Blessed's number to see where he was. If I was pregnant, it was only right that I let him know. I wasn't the type of chick to keep shit from someone until I felt like telling them. If I was going to get rid of the baby or keep it, he still was going to know it existed. I'm not saying that I was all for abortions. I thought it was fucking murder to get a baby sucked out of you. If you laid down and made the motherfucker, then you could fucking take care of it when it got here. That was just my opinion though.

"Yeah?" he answered the phone with a lot of noise in his background.

"I hate to bother you, but were you busy?"

"Not at the moment. Why what's up? You must want some more dick?" I could hear the smirk in his voice when he asked that. The noise quickly faded, letting me know he'd stepped away for some privacy.

"I need to talk to you about something that I have to do in person."

"What's it about?"

"Can you just meet me somewhere?"

"I'm at *Nova Beach*."

"Okay, I can be there in like forty-five minutes." Without giving him the chance to say anything else, I disconnected the call and grabbed the two tests, shoving them both into my pockets and rushed out of the house. I was in such a hurry that I didn't even bother to put the groceries up that I just got from the store. They were going to have to wait until I made it back home.

Pulling up at *Nova Beach*, I sat there in the car, debating on how I wanted to tell him I was pregnant. I thought of so many ways to hand him those pregnancy tests like a crazy woman. Tapping on my car window caught me off guard. I jumped and looked over straight into Blessed's face. He pulled the passenger's side door open and slipped into the seat.

"How long have you been sitting out here?" he questioned me, shutting the door.

"I don't know."

"What's wrong with you?" He shifted in his seat facing me.

"Well…" I paused for a moment, feeling as if I was about to have a panic attack. "After you left this morning, I got to feeling bad and vomiting everywhere, so I went to the store and bought a pregnancy test."

"You're not trying to tell me that you're pregnant, are you?" He chuckled, probably trying to lighten the mood. His reaction let me know that he wasn't going to be excited about it either, but we made this baby, and now it was time that we took the responsibility for it.

Reaching into my pocket, I pulled out one of the tests and laid it in his lap. His eyes darted to it and he sat there silent for a moment, terrifying me because I didn't know what was running through his mind.

"And it's mine?" he had the fucking nerves to ask me like I was some got damn hoe he'd met on the fucking streets.

"Of course, it's yours! The fuck!" My face scrunched up and I wanted to reach over there and smack the shit out of him but opted out of it.

"How I know that though?" His gaze finally met mine.

"Nigga, you been the only motherfucker I been fucking. The fuck you mean?" I smacked him in the back of his head. I couldn't believe he was asking me some bullshit like that. Whenever I was having sex with someone, I always made sure I was fucking one person at a got damn time. If I ever caught something, you better believe I was damn well going to know where the shit came from. If he was asking me something like that, that only meant he had been fucking other bitches behind my back and my assumptions were correct.

"I had to ask. Bitches lie about nigga's being their baby daddies every day."

"Well, I ain't bitches. Nigga... you are the fucking father. Question is, what the fuck you gon' do about it?"

"You keeping it?"

"Just as sure as my name is Sa'nai. If you don't want to be in the baby's life, then I can't force you to be, but if it's God's will, that baby is going to be born with or without you."

"I don't know why I thought you were going to say you were going to get an abortion or something."

"I see you tiptoeing around my question though."

I shot him daggers and he said, "If you're keeping it, I'll be here."

"Good. That's all I wanted. I'm about to go back home and get in bed."

His hand landed on my thigh and I stared down at it. "You gon' let me come over later?" he quizzed, licking his lips and my pussy tingled.

"Boy, get out of my car." A smile crept onto my lips. That's the very reason we were in this predicament.

"I take that as a yes." He grinned and climbed out of the car, shutting the door. I pulled out of that parking lot with a lot weighing heavily on my mind. My entire world was about to change before my eyes, and I didn't know what to do about it.

Sapphire

Later that day...

"**Y**ou're what!" My eyes bucked as I listened to Sa'nai on the phone. When she called me back, I thought she was going to tell me that she still wasn't feeling the best and was going to the doctor or something. I know damn well my ears were deceiving me.

"You fucking heard me, Sapphire. I really don't feel like repeating the shit, right now." From the tone of her voice, I could tell she wasn't in the best of mood about finding out she was pregnant. If she hadn't been fucking Blessed without a condom, then she wouldn't be stressing about that shit.

"I can't believe you're fucking pregnant. Did you tell him?" I quizzed her, climbing out of my car and entering the building my office was located in. I had snuck off for a little lunchtime with Kon and Stormie. She had been spending a lot of time with us lately because her mother was still pissed about Kon not wanting to be with her. Every time she got a feeling that we were together, she'd call his phone to drop his daughter off. I was beginning to see the child more than she was.

"Of course, I told him. This nigga had the fucking nerves to ask me if the baby was his. Like nigga, what type of bitch do you take me as? I'm not one of those hoes he found out there on the streets. If I'm fucking him, he the only motherfucker going in this pussy."

"I know that's real," I agreed with her. That was one thing we didn't do—go out and fuck multiple niggas at one time. Even when I was fucking Jonathan just for the hell of it, he was the only nigga I was fucking. I didn't understand how the hell some bitches could fuck two, three, or four niggas at one time like that. The shit was disgusting as fuck and they were bound to catch some shit.

I stepped off the elevator and Sasha jumped from her desk. I knew she needed to tell me something from her facial expression.

"What is it, Sasha?" I asked her, covering the phone with my hand.

"Someone has been calling the office all morning leaving death threats."

"Sa'nai, let me call you back." I ended the call, giving Sasha my undivided attention. This was the first time some-thing like that had ever happened.

"Did they say who they were?"

"No, but it's a woman's voice. I've never heard it before. I was trying to wait until you got here to see if you wanted me to call the police. I don't want anything to happen to you." Mois-ture filled her eyes. From the tears, I could tell it must have been serious.

At first thought, I thought it may have been someone who I turned down for a job or had fucked something up on their big day. Threats were nothing to take lightly, so I definitely needed to get a grip on this situation before their threats became a fuck-ing reality.

Gripping Sasha by the shoulders, I gazed into her eyes and said, "Nothing's going to happen to either of us. I'll take care of it." And released her. I wasn't sure how I was going to go about this situation, but something had to be done and quickly. "If they just so happen to call back, transfer them to my phone." Maybe if I heard the voice, I could figure out who the mother-fucker was. Either way, they were going to suffer the fucking consequences for fucking playing with me and my got damn money.

I headed into my office and shut the door behind me, re-leasing a breath I didn't even know I was holding in. Placing my things down at the desk, I grabbed my phone and went to call Kon to tell him what was going on at the office when my door burst open and Chrissy stormed in with Sasha right on her heels.

"I tried to stop her!" Sasha glanced at me with pleading eyes. I wasn't worried about her barging into my office, I was worried about how the fuck this bitch found me.

"Have you been getting my messages?"

"So that was you, playing on the fucking phone like a lit-tle ass child?"

"You want me to call the police?" Sasha quickly asked. I knew she was worried about my wellbeing, but Chrissy was the least of my fucking worries. I beat her ass before, and I'll damn sure do it again. It was best that she found something safe to fucking do.

"It's fine, Sasha; I got it."

"You sure?"

"Yes."

She shut the door behind her, and I took my eyes back to Chrissy. That motherfucker stood inches away from my desk with her arms folded across her chest.

"What the fuck are you doing here, Chrissy?"

"Did you think I was just going to calmly let you take my fucking man?"

"I didn't take anything. You're being delusional as fuck."

"You took my fucking man! You were sleeping with him behind my back and now you two are walking around rubbing the bullshit in my face like it's alright. Both of y'all gon' pay for the shit." Storming over to my shelf, she knocked down all my journals and books onto the floor. "I'm not standing by like the shit is okay anymore!" She flipped one of the chairs over in front of my desk and I bolted to my feet.

"What you not going to do is come in here and tear up my fucking office!" I stormed around my desk, pulling my jacket off dropping it on top of the desk and rolled up the sleeves on my shirt. This bitch was really pushing my buttons and she wasn't going to learn until I damn near killed her ass. I worked too fucking hard and too got damn long for her to come in here thinking she was about to destroy some shit. My career was one thing I didn't fucking play about.

"Bitch, before it's all said and done, you and Kon are going to be nonfactors."

"I'm done talking. Bring your ass on." I beckoned for her and she smiled. This bitch was about to get her ass whooped for the second time and she was fucking smiling about it. That alone let me know she was crazy as hell.

She neared me and I swung on her, hitting her dead in the chin. Her head tilted back, and she charged me like a fucking linebacker or some shit. We crashed into my desk and a few things went crashing to the floor. Not long after, the office door opened and Sasha shrieked at the top of her lungs when she saw Chrissy and I rolling around on the floor. I wasn't about to let that bitch get the best of me and I damn sure wasn't about to let her snatch any more hair out of my got damn head. I hated whenever you fought a bitch and they always went for your hair. That alone let you know the motherfucker couldn't fight.

"You can't have my fucking man!" she cried as I tried my best to get on top of her, but she had a hold on my got damn hair.

"Bitch let my fucking hair go!"

Wham!

I head-butted her and it left both of us dazed for a moment—her a little bit longer than me. I hopped on top of her and pounded her face in with my fist.

"You're not going to keep fucking disrespecting me, ho!"

Wham!

I got a few more licks in before I was pulled off of her from behind. That's when I realized Sasha must have called security. If she hadn't, I was absolutely sure I might have killed that bitch in there. I was so angry about how she came at me. I wasn't thinking about how this shit made me look or how it may have affected other people if she seriously had gotten hurt. I was tired of that bitch.

Tired of how she looked at me whenever she was near. Tired of her fucking blaming me for losing Kon. The stupid shit she did was the reason why he no longer wanted to be with her ass, not me. I may be the reason now, but I wasn't when he decided to call it quits on their relationship.

The security guard yanked Chrissy up from the floor. Her hair was all over her head and I could only imagine how mine looked. That bitch wanted to pull some more of my shit out.

"I'm not finished with your ass!" she shouted as they carried her out of the office. The other security guard released me, and I dusted my clothes off. Sasha brushed my hair down with her hands.

"Are you okay?" she questioned me.

"I will be. Just make sure to let them know downstairs that she's not allowed back into the building. If she had shown up while I had a client in there I would have been embarrassed as hell. No way was I about to let a bitch that didn't have shit going for herself, and was living off of her baby daddy, ruin shit for me.

"Will do," she said and left out of my office, shutting the door behind her.

I cleaned up everything she knocked over and took a seat back behind my desk. Scooping my phone up, I dialed Kon's number to let him know what happened. It took him a moment to answer the phone and I thought I was going to have to leave work and hunt his ass down to tell him about his stupid ass baby mama.

"Yeah, bae?" he finally answered, and normally, I'd get fucking butterflies whenever he called me that, but at the moment, heat coursed through my veins and I wanted to cause serious damage to Chrissy.

"You really need to do something with your crazy ass baby mama."

"What she did now?"

"That bitch came into my office, knocking shit over and shit. I had to beat her fucking ass. And let me not forget to tell you that all morning she had been calling leaving death threats with Sasha. You seriously need to do something with her ass before you end up being a single fucking parent. I'm not going to keep playing with her ass, Kon."

"I'll talk to her."

"You need to do more than talk. You need to knock that bitch's head between the fridge and the freezer. I'm sick of her ass, and it's only so much I'm gon' stand there and take when it comes to her."

"Bae, I told you, I'ma handle it. I have to get back to work. I'll get up with you later, aight?"

"Uh huh. You better handle that bitch. I'm not playing with you, Kon."

"Yeah," was all he said before ending the call. I was irritated as fuck at how he was all nonchalant about the situation.

NECHOL

He better had done something with that bitch before she ended up dead somewhere because I wasn't about to keep playing with her ass.

Kon

I scrubbed my hand across my mouth and sighed, slipping my phone onto the desk. That phone call with Sapphire about Chrissy weighed heavily on my mind. I thought Chrissy was done playing those childish ass games, but I was wrong. She was still holding onto the hate from when I left her and wouldn't let the shit go and move the fuck on. That was one of the many reasons why we weren't together anymore. We were getting too old for this bullshit and it had to fucking stop. If she caused me to lose Sapphire behind this bullshit, I was going to end up knocking her got damn head off.

It made me wonder how the fuck she had time to fuck with Sapphire in the first place when she was supposed to be at home with Stormie. This was her first time having her in over a week. She always seemed to have a fucking excuse as to why she had to drop her off with me. It wasn't like she had to fucking work because she hadn't had a fucking job since we first got together.

I always made sure Chrissy was straight. I bent over backward to take care of her, and now I felt like she was fucking spitting in my got damn face.

My office door burst in and I looked up into Blessed's face. He didn't seem too happy stumbling into my office. That motherfucker called me earlier while he was at the club and told me all about shorty he fucked around and knocked up. Blessed wasn't the father type of guy, so I knew he wasn't too thrilled to find out he had a baby on the way. Even though he was great when it came to Stormie, she wasn't his and he could always give her back whenever he wanted to. That baby they were about to bring into the world, he was stuck with it for the rest of his life. I'm sure once it made its grand entrance he was going to warm up to the idea and fall in love with it the same as I did mine.

"Don't tell me that you're still in your fucking feelings about Sa'nai."

"That shit ain't even on my mind, right now. I came to get you, so we could run off to the trap on Coral Gate Drive. I got a call from Don saying that we needed to get over there ASAP."

"What the fuck do you think could have happened?"

"I don't know, but I do think we need to hurry up and get over there to see what the fuck is going on. Whatever it is, he didn't want to say over the phone."

Rising to my feet, I grabbed my gun off the desk and tucked it into my waistline. Dealing with Chrissy's foolishness was going to have to wait until I saw what the fuck was going on at my trap.

Lately, everything had been running smoothly for me except for when that new motherfucker popped up on the got damn map. Blessed was supposed to be working on finding out who the motherfucker was and what the fuck he wanted, but so far, he'd come up empty-handed.

I knew that motherfucker was going to be a problem as soon as Blessed brought that bullshit to me. Without a doubt, whatever happened at my trap, I was positive that motherfucker had something to do with the shit.

I hopped into the car and sped all the way to Coral Gate Drive. When we arrived, Don was standing on the porch, scrolling on his phone. He should have had his ass out trying to see what the fuck was going on instead of being all on Snap Chat and shit. This trap was his fucking responsibility and he was calling us crying about some shit that he was supposed to have taken care of himself.

Getting out of the car, we approached the house and he quickly put his phone away.

"What the fuck happened?" I asked him, climbing the couple of steps to the porch.

"I ran off right quick and when I came back, shit was like this," he answered, pushing the door open for us. We entered the house and I saw two niggas lying on the living room floor with bullet holes in their foreheads. Their guns weren't too far from their bodies, but if both of them were taken down, they might have gotten caught off guard.

Stepping over the bodies, I walkeded towards the kitchen and all the girls that worked at this trap were sprawled out on the floor with puddles of blood around them.

"Is anything missing?"

I noticed the empty containers on the counter where the cocaine was supposed to be. I just knew in my fucking gut that they took every got damn thing out of there.

"Everything's gone," Don answered, and I wanted to smack the shit out of him. For whatever reason, I felt like some shit was off. Don never left his post during the day unless it was something extremely important or one of us called him.

"Where the fuck was you?" I asked, closing in on him and he backed into Blessed.

"I had to run off to the hospital. My baby mama called and told me that Junior was in the emergency room," he quickly answered without hesitation, but I still felt like something wasn't right.

"Aight. Blessed, see what the fuck you can come up. Don,

call the clean-up crew. Once shit dies down, I'll send another crew over here." I wasn't about to place any more of my fucking crew or product in this got damn house until I knew for fucking sure what the fuck was going on. I just lost out on a shit load of money and damn sure wasn't about to do the shit again.

Blessed nodded and walked back out the door. I took one final glance around the house, and sighed. A war was about to break out. I could feel the shit in my bones and I damn sure wasn't prepared for one. I'd been running Miami for the longest with the help of Blessed and didn't have to worry about a fucking war because no one was stupid enough to start some shit with us. That nigga that appeared out of thin air, he had to be from somewhere else because he was beyond ready to go six feet under.

I exited out of the house and Blessed was ending a phone call. Since he rode over to the trap with me, I had to drop him off at his car before I went over Chrissy's house and shoved my fucking foot up her ass.

"I think I have a lead," he said, hopping into the car alongside me.

"Good. The quicker we get rid of this motherfucker, the quicker shit can go back to normal. I'm about to drop you back off at your car. I have to go take care of something with Chrissy."

"Is everything alright with her?" he swiftly asked. I knew he was probably worried about Stormie, but the problem I had with my baby mama had nothing to do with our daughter.

"For the moment, yeah, but when I get my fucking hands on her ass, it won't be."

"What she did now?"

"That motherfucker went up to Sapphire's job and cut the fuck up. I don't know what the hell to do with her ass at this point. I've given her everything I possibly could, and she's still not satisfied."

"Then you're just going to have to just let her ass go and find her way on her own. She's no longer your responsibility, Kon. The only person you're supposed to be taking care of is Stormie. If I were you, I'd cut ties with her ass. Maybe she'd get some act right then."

"We'll see."

At this point, I wasn't sure what was going to work with Chrissy. One moment she's fine with the breakup, then the next, she's doing everything in her fucking power to try and end shit between Sapphire and I, I just want peace.

After dropping Blessed off at his car, I went straight to Chrissy's house. She was there because her car was parked in the driveway. Getting out of the car, I went up to the front door and went to unlock it, but my fucking key didn't work.

"What the fuck?"

Boom! Boom! Boom!

I bang rapidly on the front door. Chrissy had me fucked up. That bitch went and changed the got damn locks on my ass to keep me out.

"Chrissy!" I barked at the top of my lungs.

Boom! Boom! Boom!

It took her a moment, but she finally came to the door with a scowl on her face.

"What the fuck do you want?"

I realized she had a couple of bruises on her face. That's what the fuck she got for going over there fucking with Sapphire in the first place.

"Why the fuck my key don't work?"

"Do you live here, nigga?" Her head cocked to the side and

eyes bucked. I wanted to knock those shits to the back of her fucking head, but I wasn't the type to put my hands on women. If my mama even heard about me placing my hands on a woman, she'd fly over to my house, and beat the dog shit out of my ass.

"I still pay the bills in this motherfucker."

"And?"

I shoved past her into the house and she turned, leaning into the door.

"Is that all you wanted because I do have shit to do."

"Since fucking when?"

"I do have a life you know..."

"And what does that fucking consist of? You going to people's jobs and tryna destroy everything they built?"

"That bitch had that shit coming with her homewrecking ass. Don't tell me that's why you brought your ass all the way over here."

"Look, I don't know what the fuck your problem is, but you're going to have to stay the fuck away from Sapphire."

"Or else?" A smile emerged onto her face and I wanted to slap the shit right off. Chrissy knew what the fuck she was doing. That motherfucker was trying her best to piss me the fuck off.

Stepping closer to her, she didn't budge. I don't know where the fuck she got her newfound balls from, but if she kept fucking with me, I was going to rip those motherfuckers right off and shove them down her got damn throat.

"Keep fucking playing with me, Chrissy. I'm sick of these fucking temper tantrums you been throwing out the got damn blue. And I'm fucking tired of you picking on Sapphire. I know you're tired of getting your fucking ass whooped. I'm not going to tell you to leave her the fuck alone again. If some shit like this happens again, you're cut the fuck off."

"You can't be serious right now!" she shouted, releasing the door. "After all the shit I put up with over the last nine years, you're really ready to choose this bitch over me? We got fucking history. You've known this hoe... what? Five minutes and you ´re prepared to throw every fucking thing away for this bitch?"

"Watch your fucking mouth, Chrissy." My jaw muscles tightened. I understood she was hurting, but that didn't give her the fucking right to keep disrespecting Sapphire as if she had done something to her ass. We were broken up because of her actions. The shit was a long time coming before Sapphire even came into the fucking picture.

"Know what, get the fuck out of my house!"

"I'm leaving, but the next time I come back, those fucking locks better be changed back."

"Fuck you, Kon!" she screamed behind me and slammed the door. Chrissy was mad as fuck now, but soon she'd get over the shit, or at least I hoped she would.

Sa'nai

A couple of days later...

S hit was still surreal to know that I was pregnant. Even after sitting on the shit for a few days, I still couldn't believe it. Blessed seemed to act a little bit different toward me now that he knew he had a baby on the way.

Today, he was supposed to have met me in my classroom for lunch. I didn't want anything to eat, but I did want some dick and was excited about the shit, but he never showed. That was the first time he'd ever blew me off and didn't answer the phone. It had me wondering if this was what I was supposed to look forward to since I was pregnant.

If he didn't want to come, then he should have just fucking said that this morning when I texted him about the shit. We were texting back and forth, and he said a few dirty things to me that had my mind wandering. I burst out and asked him to come by on my planning period, so we could both relieve some stress. I noted how stressed he had been the last couple of days. He didn't really tell me what was going on; he never did when it came to his work, but I was worried about him. Too much stress could kill a person or land them in the hospital.

The bell rang, grasping my attention and I stood to my feet and walked my children outside. I stood there, saying goodbye to every single one of them until they all were gone.

"Is everything okay?" Mrs. Berkley asked as I was entering

the building to straighten up my classroom and gather my belongings. She and I weren't really friends. She was older than me and Caucasian, but she was sweet as can be.

"Yes, it's fine. Thanks for asking." I trekked down the hallway to my classroom and began to clean up. Blessed seeped into my mind again and I couldn't get rid of him for the life of me.

Grabbing my phone, I tried calling him again, but this time he sent me straight to voicemail. He was really starting to piss me the fuck off. I've never gone this long without hearing something back from him, even if it was a text letting me know he was busy or something.

Using the find my phone application, I searched for his phone and it popped up showing that he was at this restaurant that I had Sapphire meet me at a while ago. He had time to go out to fucking eat, but the bitch couldn't answer the fucking phone for me. Bet.

I finished up my classroom and rushed outside to my car. I checked the application again and he was still in the same spot.

"Let's see what has you so fucking busy."

I drove all the way to __ to see if Blessed was still there. When I arrived, his car was sitting almost by the door. Anger consumed me as I pulled into the parking lot and parked my car. I sat there for a moment, waiting to see if he was going to come out, and who may have been with him. My mind was all over the place because I knew if he was at a restaurant like that during the day, he had to have a bitch with him.

We weren't officially together, but I at least thought he would have let it be known that he was seeing other people. And if he had other plans already, he should have made that clear before we schedule our little session.

After sitting in the car for fifteen minutes and there was no sign of him, I decided to get out of the car and go inside to see what the fuck was going on. Entering the building, my eyes scanned it, searching for Blessed.

"Can I help you?" the hostess asked, grasping my attention. Unless she knew where the fuck Blessed was and why the hell he blew me off, then she couldn't do a damn thing for me.

"I'm looking for someone."

"What's their name. Maybe I can help you find them."

My eyes locked with hers and I said, "Blessed."

"Oh, right this way."

I followed closely behind her through the restaurant and my eyes landed on the back of his head. He was facing me, and some chick was sitting directly in front of him with a huge smile on her fucking face. I don't know how the hell I knew that was his ass, but I fucking knew it. Heat coursed through my head and I thought of all types of ways I was going to beat his ass once my hands landed on him.

"You son of a bitch." I power walked to where he sat and slammed my hands down on the table.

Boom!

The girl sitting across from him jumped.

"Is this why you haven't been answering the fucking phone?" My eyes locked with his and he wore a scowl. I don't give a damn if he was in his fucking feelings about me popping up on his ass, he shouldn't have ever fucking stood me up.

"This isn't the time or place for that shit, Sa'nai."

"Who is she?" the chick questioned him.

"His girlfriend. Who the fuck are you?" My head cocked to the side. I could only imagine how Blessed was looking at the moment. We never agreed on what we were to each other. In fact, the shit never came up. We were just going with the flow, but now that I was pregnant, I was taking the fucking title of being his girl whether he wanted me to or not.

"Uh, Stephanie," she almost hesitated. From her facial expression, I could tell she was uncomfortable as hell. "I think I should go." She rose to her feet.

"No!" Blessed barked, stopping her in her tracks.

"No!" My head quickly snapped in his direction. "What the fuck you mean, no!"

Blessed bolted to his feet and swiftly grabbed me by the arm, dragging me away from the table.

"I don't know why you coming up in here starting shit." He pulled me out of the door and slung me in front of him.

"Why the hell you stood me up? Are you fucking her or something?" Tears filled my eyes and I hated that shit. I didn't want to cry in front of him. I didn't want him to know that it bothered me more than it should have.

"Hell no, and I forgot to call you to let you know I wasn't going to make it."

"Why? Because you were too busy thinking about fucking her?"

"It ain't nothing like that. She had me meet her here to talk about some shit that happened the other day. I was actually getting some intel out of her before you showed up."

"It didn't look like it to me. From the smile on her fucking face, it looked like she wanted to fuck your ass."

"If she do, I don't have shit to do with it. You're the only motherfucker I'm worried about right now."

I chewed on the inside of my jaw to keep myself from smiling.

Closing in on me, he gripped me by the waist and pulled

me into his frame. I gazed up into his eyes.

"Why I feel like you're bullshitting with me right now?"

He cupped my chin and stared directly into my eyes. "I don't have a reason to do that. I like you, Sa'nai and according to you, you're my girl." The corner of his lips curved into a smirk.

"You do realize that means you have to let go of all those bitches you been fucking with."

"The only motherfucker I been fucking is you and I'm surprised my damn self."

"Are you going to tell me what's going on with that bitch in there?" I pointed my thumb over my shoulder. I know he said she had something to do with something what happened the other day, but that still wasn't explaining shit to me.

"It's best that you don't know."

"What's that supposed to mean?"

"Don't worry your pretty little head about it."

Pulling his phone out of his pocket, he gazed at the time and said, "I have to get back in there, but if you're not busy by the time I'm done, I promise to come make it up to you."

"Is that so?" A smile passed my lips. It was crazy how just that fucking fast, I was no longer angry with him anymore.

"Yup." His hands cupped my ass and his lips found mine.

"Long as you don't fucking stand me up again," I said when I pulled back.

"I'ma come running; I promise."

Blessed

I had forgotten all about getting up with Sa'nai during her planning period. I didn't think she would hunt me down and cause a scene the way she had. Sa'nai didn't seem like that type of chick, but any bitch would cut the fuck up if she was sprung off the dick.

Honestly, my mind was all over the fucking place. I had so much to do that it was a fucking shame. Kon was on my ass about me finding out who that motherfucker Thugga was. That was the whole point in me meeting with this chick. She was one of his workers and I was trying my best to flip her ass to give me some sort of information that I could use against the mother-fucker.

When she first arrived, she didn't want to talk about Thugga. I had to bribe the motherfucker with cash and ensure her a position on the team after we got rid of his ass. I really didn't even know how the fuck he got in our city and set up shop without us even fucking knowing it.

"Sorry about that," I apologized to her and took my seat back.

"It's fine. I totally understand."

She toyed with her food, looking uncomfortable as hell. I really wished Sa'nai hadn't shown up when she did.

I took a sip from my drink, eyeing the shit out of her. "I think you're not telling me everything."

She told me about the trap where she worked and how many people were in there, but I still felt like she knew more than what she was telling. I didn't want to retaliate by hitting one of their spots. I wanted to do something bigger to show that nigga that this was our fucking city and he better pack up and get the fuck on before he found himself six feet under.

"I told you everything I know." She kept her eyes fixated on her plate. That was a sign that she was lying. She couldn't even look me in the got damn face. I'm not sure what the fuck she was so afraid of, I told her that I'd protect her if she worked with me.

"Stephanie." My hand covered hers and she brought her watery eyes up to mine. "I promise you don't have anything to worry about if you just tell me what I need to know."

Her teeth sank into the corner of her lower lip as her eyes searched mine. "Alright, but you didn't hear this from me."

"What is it?" I pulled my hand away from hers and relaxed back in my seat.

"Thugga has a shipment coming in, in a few days. I know about it because he wanted me to be there at the warehouse to test the product."

"And you couldn't start with this shit? The entire fucking warehouse and shipment are more important than a fucking trap. They took all our shit from our trap. How about we take all of their fucking shipment?" A smirk formed on my face. I was already trying to think of a plan on how I was going to get my hands on his shit and get it off as quickly as possible. I didn't give a damn if he knew we were the ones that took his shit. In fact, I wanted his ass to know, so he'd think twice about fucking with us again. No shipment meant that he didn't have any product and he would have to work twice as hard to get a new one or just give up altogether.

"Do you really think that's a good idea?"

"Why wouldn't it be?"

"I just think that it's going to be dangerous as fuck."

"You don't have to worry about us. We got all this shit under control. You just let me know what day the shipment is going down, and I'll be there."

"If Thugga finds out—"

"He won't unless you go running your mouth."

I raised my hand for the check and the waitress came right over. "Just don't fuck me over because if you do, then you'll have even bigger problems than Thugga finding out that you sold his bitch ass out."

Reaching into my pocket, I pulled out a wad of cash and tossed two-hundred dollars on the table and rose to my feet.

"I'll be in touch with you soon." I flashed her a smile and got the hell out of there.

As I headed to the car, I dialed Kon's number to let him know what I got out of Stephanie. I was beyond ready to get the fuck out of there with her and go find Sa'nai to relieve some of the stress built up inside me.

"Yeah?" he answered.

"I just met with this chick, Stephanie."

"What happened?"

"She told me about this shipment Thugga has coming in soon. She's supposed to get back with me about the details."

"Let me know soon as you find out."

"Bet." I ended the call and hopped into the car. I sped all the way over to Sa'nai's, so she'd know I wasn't lying about coming over there. I'd hate to see how she'd react if I didn't show up for a second time. She was ready to shove her foot up Stephanie's ass thinking that I was fucking the girl.

Pulling into the parking lot, I got out of the car and went into the building. When I got up to her door, I used the key she gave me and let myself inside. Slow music could be heard coming from her bedroom, so I followed the tunes and saw that she was in the bathroom.

Before I could make it to the door, she emerged, and a huge smile spread across her face when her eyes landed on me.

"About damn time." She ran over to me, jumping into my arms. The towel that was wrapped around her, dropped to the floor.

"I'm sorry about earlier." Apologizing for shit wasn't in my nature, but I knew I had to for her.

"It's okay. You're here now." She kissed me on the corner of my mouth.

I carried her over to the bed, placing her gently down on her back. She lifted onto her elbows, staring up at me. I got down on my knees, pulling her to the edge of the bed. I gazed down at her pretty pink pussy and licked my lips.

Sa'nai's shit was always sweet whenever I ate her. I don't know if it was because of all the water she drunk and fruit she ate or what, but it was some of the best pussy I ate in my life.

Sucking her clit into my mouth, I released it and she moaned, falling against the bed, covering her eyes with her arm.

"Why your shit taste so good?"

I spread her lips with my middle and index finger, swiftly licking her clit with the tip of my tongue. I kept licking, speeding up the pace and her legs shuddered, letting me know that she was close to climaxing.

"Fuuuck!" she cried out, tightly gripping the sheets. She grinded her pussy against my face and released her juices, screaming at the top of her lungs.

Licking up all her juices, I rose to my feet and wiped my mouth with the back of my hand. Shoving my pants and boxer briefs down, I stepped out of my pants.

"Toot that ass up," I instructed her, and she just laid there. I knew she was drained from the orgasm I'd just given her, but I wasn't done with that ass. She had to cum at least two more times before she was off the hook. That motherfucker wanted the dick and that's exactly what I was about to give her ass.

Gripping her by the arm, I yanked her ass up and turned her around. She got on her knees and I bit down into her ass cheek.

"Ouch!" she cried out and laughed.

"That's for not doing what I told your ass to do."

I slapped my dick against her ass and slid it up and down her slit.

"Stop teasing me," she whined as I placed my head at her opening.

I gently eased inside of her and my shit fit her like a fucking glove. "Toss that ass back."

She threw her ass back on my dick, matching my rhythm. I planted kisses on her shoulder, wrapping her hair around my hand. Sa'nai's pussy was so got damn good, that's how I fucked around and ended up knocking her ass up in the first place. The shit was so amazing that it was hard as fuck for me to pull out. I didn't even think to ask if she was on birth control or anything.

Her pussy muscles contracted, and that shit drove me fucking crazy every single time she did that shit.

"This your dick and you better not ever forget this shit," I told her, pounding my dick deep inside her.

"Shiiiiiiit!" I felt her nectar release on my dick and a smirk formed on my face.

"That's it," I coached her.

Releasing her hair, I gripped her by the neck, pulling her head back and bit her on the ear. I felt my climax reaching it's peak. Gripping her by the waist, I released my seeds deep off in her and she collapsed against the bed face first. From her panting, I knew she was tired as fuck. Shit, I'd just given myself a damn good ass workout as well.

Treading into the bathroom, I grabbed a wet rag and cleaned myself off, then cleaned her up as well. I was tired as fuck and all I wanted to do was take a nap. When I got up from my nap, I'd hop in the shower and get back to work.

$\mathcal{K}on$

The next day...

I sat there behind my desk, rubbing my temples. A few more of my people had come up dead in the streets and we had yet done anything to retaliate. The shit was pissing me the fuck off because that motherfucker Thugga was trying to show me that he wasn't going anywhere, and he was coming for my head. If that plan Blessed was coming up with didn't work, I wasn't sure what the fuck we were going to do.

I had given Don the go to sweep that nigga's trap, but that wasn't enough for me. I needed to do something bigger and better to get back at his ass. It was as if he had everything fucking planned out already and I wasn't even sure how the fuck he was finding all my shit in the first place.

I had been sitting there at my desk for the last twenty minutes trying to figure out how the fuck all this shit was happening to me. The only logical explanation was that someone had to be feeding that nigga information. The question was... who.

For the longest I've been running the streets, I thought that my entire team was fucking airtight. I guess sometimes people showed disloyalty whenever they were offered a little bit of cash. As soon as I figured out which one of those motherfuckers were snitching, I had a fucking bullet with their got damn name on it.

My phone rang, bringing me from my thoughts. Scooping it from the desk, I glanced down at the name flashing on the screen. I had been waiting on this phone call for the longest. Quickly, I swiped the screen and answered.

"About fucking time. I hope you're calling with good news."

"Your house is ready," Amber answered, putting a huge smile on my face. I was tired of staying in that fucking hotel room.

"Are you there now?" I asked her, getting up from my seat.

"Yeah. I can wait until you get here."

"Give me a couple of hours," I told her and ended the call.

Amber was the interior designer I hired to get my new house in order. I didn't want the fucking burden of trying to decorate my damn self. I was positive that Stormie was going to be excited as hell when she found out that I moved into a new house.

Heading out of the warehouse, I hopped into my car and went straight to Sapphire's job. I had been keeping from her that I had been looking for a house and was excited to let her know that I finally got one.

I made sure the house was big enough for me and Stormie, and whenever Sapphire wanted to stay the night. Eventually, I hoped she'd move in with me, but I wasn't trying to rush shit. I was trying to take my time with her, so that shit didn't end up how it did with Chrissy.

Pulling up to the building, I left the car parked at the door and went up to her office floor. Sasha smiled when her eyes landed on me as I stepped off the elevator.

"Hey, Kon," she said with a huge smile on her face.

"Is she in?" I asked, nodding in the direction of the office.

"Yeah, she's in there. She's eating lunch right now."

"Thanks."

I knocked on the door and entered, shutting it behind me. Sapphire gazed up at me with her mouth filled with fries. She hurried up and chewed and swallowed.

"I didn't know you were coming by today."

"I wasn't, but I wanted to show you something." Rushing over to her desk, I spun her around to where she was facing me.

"Show me what?" Grabbing her burger, she took a bite from it.

"It's a surprise. Come on." I pulled her up from the chair and she grabbed her food off the desk.

"You couldn't wait until I was done eating?"

Sapphire wasn't the type to pass up on a meal. She loved to eat as much as the next person. As much junk as she ate, I was surprised she hadn't packed on a few pounds. Lately, she was eating a little bit more than normal.

"I don't know what you have to do after lunch, so it's best that we go on now." I dragged her out of the office while she stuffed her mouth with food and struggled to keep up behind me.

Opening the passenger's door on my car, I waited until she was securely inside before shutting the door and rounding to my side to get in. I gazed over at her and said, "You waste that shit in my car, you gon' be cleaning it up."

"Shut up." She laughed it off, but I was serious as hell. I didn't even allow Stormie to eat in my car for those purposes.

I drove us to my new house as she sat there silently eating her food. Pulling up to the gate, I punched the code in, and her eyes darted in my direction.

"What are we doing here?"

"I told you I had something to show you," I stated again, pulling into the u-shaped driveway and parking behind Amber's Tesla.

Climbing out of the car, I rounded to her side and opened the door. "Whose house is this?" she asked, getting out glancing up at the mini-mansion. The house was almost the size of the old one, but I didn't want to do too much with this one. The only reason the other house was so fucking huge was because Chrissy was adamant about getting that particular house. When she saw that it sat on the beach, she was fucking sold. This one may not have been on the beach, but it was down the street from one, and that's something I preferred better.

Amber swung the wooden double doors open and a huge smile graced her face.

"Okay, are you going to tell me what the hell is going on?"

"I bought a house."

"You didn't!" Her eyes lit up, and she turned facing the house. From the gaze she gave it, I could tell she loved it. Her loving the house was vital if I was going to eventually ask her to move in with me.

"What do you think?"

"It's huge for just you and Stormie."

"I know..." I stepped in front of her and her gaze met mine again. "I plan on eventually asking you to move in with me. I know it's probably too soon now, but we'll get there. I just wanted to make sure that you loved the house."

"Can I see the inside?"

"It's ready," Amber added, grasping both of our attention. "I tried my best to accommodate both of you even though I had very little to go on."

Gripping her hand, I pulled her toward the front door, and she fell silent. The last time I stepped foot in this house was when I closed on it. It was empty as fuck, but judging from the looks of things, Amber did a damn good job at filling it and making it feel like a home.

Entering the foyer, I followed her into the living room. The motherfucker was all-black with a hint of gold. It had this long black sectional along the far wall. A mini gold bar sat in the corner.

She took us on a short tour of the first floor that consisted of the kitchen, family room, and office. The backyard was huge as fuck, almost never-ending. From the huge smile on Sapphire's face, I could tell she was loving it so far.

We followed Amber upstairs to, and she showed me Stormie's bedroom. It was the first door on the right. I'm glad I left her to decorate it because if it was up to me, that big ass room would have been plain and empty as fuck.

"Stormie's going to love this," Sapphire said, touching the pole of the canopy bed.

"If you think that's something, just wait until you see the master."

Amber led us out of the room and down the hallway to a set of white double doors. "You ready?" she asked with a grin over her shoulder.

"Just show me already." Sapphire was anxious as fuck. I could tell she was probably going to spend most of her time here with me.

Amber pushed the doors open and Sapphire's mouth dropped to the floor. "It's beautiful." Releasing my hand, she stepped into the bedroom and gave herself a mini-tour.

The huge gold California King bed sat in the center of the floor looking as if it weighed a fucking ton. There was a huge flat screen on the wall directly in front of it. In the right corner was a gold and white vanity where Sapphire could do her makeup whenever she came over. There were two separate walk-in closets. One was filled with clothes and shoes for me, and the other, I had Amber go out and buy some things for Sapphire. She'd no longer have to pack an overnight bag whenever she wanted to stay over—everything she'd need would be within reach.

I thought about going on and asking her to move in with me. I knew the house was going to feel empty as fuck whenever she or Stormie wasn't there. But asking her to move in would be too soon for us. I was trying to do whatever possible not to ruin this relationship.

Sapphire went on into the bathroom and I asked Amber to leave. She nodded and exited out of the bedroom shutting the door behind her. Sauntering into the bathroom, I found Sapphire standing in the mirror, taking a picture, so I stepped up behind her. My hand wrapped around her waist, pulling her tightly into my frame, and I kissed her softly on the side of her neck.

"You like the house?" I asked and she turned around, facing me.

"I love it. You really didn't have to do all that though."

"I know... I wanted to."

My hands trailed down, cupping her ass and she smirked up at me. Sapphire's ass was so fat and juicy, I could barely keep my hands off of it. Her hand reached down, stroking my dick through my jeans and the motherfucker automatically bricked up.

"Maybe you should tell her to leave," she said, nodding her head in the direction of the bedroom.

"Way ahead of you." I grinned, and our lips collided.

Gripping her by the ass, I lifted her and sat her down on the counter. I pulled her blouse over her head and tossed it to the floor. Unclamping her bra in the front, her breasts bounced. Licking my lips, I firmly gripped one, swirling my tongue around the nipple and sucked it into my mouth. A moan escaped her lips and her head tilted back. Groping her other breast, I gently sank my teeth down into her nipple and she squirmed.

Undoing her pants, I gripped them and her panties, tugging on them. She lifted and I pulled them off, dropping them to the floor. Her beautiful bald pussy stared back at me and I couldn't wait to dive into that motherfucker.

Pulling her to the edge of the counter, I spread her legs as far as they would go and latched onto her clit. She tightly gripped the counter and moaned a soft melody in my ear that turned me the fuck on even more. My tongue swiftly stroked her clit and her body shuddered.

"Give me what I want," I encouraged her.

"Fuuuck!" she cried out and her juices seeped into my mouth.

Licking her clean, I stood to my feet and shoved my pants and boxer briefs to the floor. Placing my dick at her opening, I prepared myself to enter her. Her nails dug deep into my shoulder and I gently eased the tip in and out of her.

I dropped my dick off inside her. Gripping her waist, I lifted her from the counter and pounded inside her.

"Shiiiit!" she hissed, and her teeth sank into her lower lip.

Sapphire's pussy was good as fuck, I always had to take my mind to another place, so I didn't end up cumming too fucking fast. She had a nigga second guessing his stamina around this bitch.

I lifted her all the way to the tip and her eyes peeled open. I slammed her straight down on my dick, and she cried out in pleasure and pain. A few more strokes and I yanked her off my dick, planting her on her feet.

"Turn around," I instructed her, and she did as she was told. I pushed her over the counter, and she lifted a little bit on her tippy toes.

Smack!

I slapped her on the ass, and it jiggled. That shit turned me on even more. Placing my dick at her entrance, I slapped it against her and shoved it inside.

"Throw that ass back on that dick."

Our skin smacked together making this melody. Her head tilted back against my chest, and I wrapped my hand around her throat.

"I love the shit out of you, girl." Before she could respond, I shoved my tongue into her mouth, realizing what I'd just told her. That was my first time saying that shit out loud to her. I didn't know if I said it because I was wrapped up in the moment or what, but the shit was out there, and I couldn't take it back.

"Ungh, I'm about to cum," she moaned, panting.

I swiftly massaged her clit, so she'd climax at the exact time as me.

"Fuuuuck, Kon!" she cried out, releasing her juices. I dumped my seeds deep off inside her and pulled out. Treading over to the linen closet, I grabbed us both a towel and started the shower.

We cleaned up in silence and got back dressed. I had to get her back to her job, so she could get back to work. We made plans to get up with each other later for dinner and went our separate ways.

Sapphire

The next day...

I hadn't been feeling the best, so I decided to stay home from work. I was going to work from home, but I could barely get my ass up out of the bed. Kon had called me earlier to check on me, and volunteered to come by and take care of me, but I told him that I'll be fine.

Whenever I got sick, I wanted to be to myself until I got better. Most people be wanting others to take care of them, but I wasn't most people.

The entire day, I laid in bed not being able to get up and eat anything. I tried to eat crackers and I wasn't even able to keep those down either.

Groaning, I turned over in bed and faced the wall, holding my stomach. It was empty to the fucking max, but I wouldn't dare try to put anything on it.

"What the hell are you in here doing?" Sa'nai's voice caught me off guard.

"What are you doing here?" I turned over, facing the doorway where she was standing. She was still dressed up, so I knew she must have come straight to my house after getting off work. I didn't even call and tell her that I wasn't feeling well, so this visit was unexpected.

"Kon called and asked if I could come check on you. I

asked him for what, then he told me that you were sick. I was like, no not my bitch. She would have called and told me." She neared the bed with a scowl on her face. "You mind telling me how come you didn't let me know that you were sick?"

"It's nothing. I didn't want to worry you for no reason. I woke up not feeling too well and said that if it got worse, I was just going to make a doctor's appointment to see what's going on."

"Well, you might as well call the doctor because I'm not leaving him until I know what the fuck is going on with you." From her facial expression, I could tell she was serious as a fucking heart attack.

"I think I might have the flu or something."

"That's an even better reason for you to take your ass to the doctor." Rounding my bed, she grabbed my phone off the nightstand and handed it over to me. "Call your fucking doctor."

Sighing, I sat up in bed, brushing my loose strands of hair back out of my face and snatched my phone away from her.

"I don't care about you being fucking mad. Your ass laying up in here sick and shit. If you don't go see what the fuck is wrong with you, you'll just end up getting worse."

She went over to my dresser and searched through my clothes for something for me to put on while I called my doctor and told them my symptoms over the phone. Lucky for me, they had a cancellation and could fit me into the schedule.

Sa'nai tossed some clothes on the bed and stood there with her arms folded over her chest.

"Can I at least get cleaned up first? I took a shower last night, but I need to take one this morning."

"Go ahead; I'm not stopping you." She flopped down on the foot of the bed and pulled out her phone.

It took everything in me to pull myself to my feet and drag them to the bathroom. I turned on the shower and waited until the water was at the perfect temperature before stripping out of my clothes and stepping inside.

I hurried up and took my shower not knowing when the next wave of nausea was going to hit me like a ton of bricks. I probably should have been got up and went to the doctor when I wasn't able to eat my saltine crackers. Sitting in there most of the day starving to death wasn't a great feeling at all.

Stepping out of the shower, I wrapped a towel around me and went into the bedroom. Sa'nai was engrossed in a conversation on the phone and from the huge ass smile resting on her face, I could tell she was probably talking to Blessed´s ass. More and more each day, I see them blossoming as a couple and I loved that shit for her.

While she talked on the phone, I got dressed and brushed my hair up into a ponytail.

"I'm ready," I told her, grasping her attention.

"I have to go, Blessed. I'll hit you up when I'm done with Sapphire." Ending her call, she grabbed her purse and keys off the bed and rose to her feet. We left out of the house and I made sure to lock up behind me.

When we got to the doctor´s, it was packed as hell in there. Sa'nai and I sat in the waiting room for at least an hour. It pissed me the fuck off because when they give me a time to be there, I expect to be called at that fucking time, not fucking forty-minutes later. That was one of the reasons why I hated going to the doctor and tried my best to only go if I really needed to.

"Sapphire Snow!" the nurse called out my name, and I rose to my feet.

"I'll wait out here until you're done," Sa'nai said, and I

nodded.

I followed the nurse to the back. She weighed me and then took me into one of the exam rooms. I sat there, fidgeting with my fingers as she set up the machine to take my temperature and pressure.

"What brings you in today?"

"I haven't been feeling well all morning. I think I might have the flu or something. Nothing I eat will stay down."

"Well, you don't have a fever." She signed into the computer and took a look at my file. "It says that you haven't gotten your birth control pills refilled in a month."

"Are you serious? I could have sworn I just filled those pills." I sat there wracking my brain, trying to remember the last time I took my birth control pills. I couldn't even remember.

"I think we should take a pregnancy test to rule it out."

"I can't be pregnant."

"We'll see. Pee in this cup for me." Reaching underneath the counter, she pulled out a plastic cup and handed it over to me. When I woke up this morning not feeling the best, the possibility of being pregnant never crossed my mind. I had been having so much fun with Kon lately, that I was slipping from my responsibilities.

Taking the cup, I went to the nearest bathroom and peed in it. I sat there for a moment, staring at my pee, praying the test was negative. I was reaching a peak in my career and just didn't think that a baby was good for me at the moment. There was still so much more shit I wanted to accomplish before I even thought about having a child. That's the reason why I was on birth control in the first place.

"Are you okay in there?" someone knocked on the door and asked. I hadn't realized how long I had been in the bathroom until the nurse came looking for me.

Getting up from the toilet, I grabbed the cup and took it out of the bathroom, handing it to her. I didn't even wait around to see what she had to say, I went back to the room and sat down on the table. Nibbling on my fingernails, I sat there anxiously waiting to see what they had to say about my results.

A knock at the door caught my attention and Doctor George entered the room with a smile on his face. Every time I saw that man, he was smiling and shit. No way anyone on this earth was that got damn happy.

"Hey, Ms. Snow. How are you feeling today?"

"Awful," I answered, waiting for him to get to the got damn point. He was going to drive me insane if he didn't tell me what I needed to know.

"I'm sorry to hear that. Vanessa made you do a pregnancy test and I just wanted to say congratulations. You're pregnant."

I bit down hard on the inside of my jaw that I could have sworn I tasted blood.

"Doesn't look like you're excited about that."

I sat there staring into space worried about how this was going to affect my career. How being pregnant was going to change my life, and I'm not sure if it's in a good way. I didn't even know how Kon was going to react to the news. Sure, he already had a daughter, but that didn't mean he wanted other children. All I could think about was the negative.

The doctor kept on talking, telling me shit I needed to do since I was pregnant, but I basically tuned all of that shit out. He told me there were options if I didn't want to keep the baby myself. Abortion was out of the fucking question. Whatever I was going to do, I had to consult with Kon first to see where his head was at.

I shook his hand and left out of the room, trying to figure

out my next move. My mind was all over the fucking place at the moment. Sa'nai knew it because she rushed over to me soon as her eyes landed on me.

"What happened?" she quickly asked, grabbing me by the forearm, pulling me toward the exit.

We got outside and I just stood there with moisture filled eyes, gazing back at her.

"Sapphire?" She lightly shook me, trying to gain my attention and get me to say something.

"I'm-I'm pregnant," I stammered over my words still not believing the shit that seeped from my lips. How the fuck did I let this shit happen?

"That's great news isn't it?" Her brow rose as she waited for me to respond to her. In her eyes, it may have been. She would no longer be pregnant by herself and would have someone to go through the different stages of pregnancy with.

"I don't think I'm ready for a child right now, Sa'nai."

"Why not? I've always told you that you'd make a great mother whenever the time presented itself. Sure, it may have come at a time that you weren't expecting, but that doesn't make my statement any less true."

"But my career…" My lower lip quivered as I saw it demolish before my eyes.

"There's plenty of women who have children and still have a successful career. Shit look at Beyoncé. That motherfucker got three of them and she still successful as shit. Just take some time to think about it. Don't make any decisions right now that you might regret later."

She pulled me to the car and opened the passenger's door for me. I slid into the seat and sat there, staring straight ahead wandering how my conversation was going to go with Kon once I told him what I found out.

Sa'nai dropped me off at the house and I hopped into my car to go and see Kon. He told me he was home because Chrissy had dropped Stormie off with him and he couldn't do much with his daughter being around.

I made it to his house and climbed out of the car. Using the key he gave me, I entered and took a deep breath.

"Kon!" I called out his name to see where he was. With how weak I felt, I damn sure didn't feel like going around this entire house just to fucking search for him. Pulling my phone out, I dialed his number and my heart pounded in my chest with every ring of the phone.

"I'm in the family room."

"Okay."

Taking deep breaths, I made my way toward the family room. With each step I took, it felt like I was carrying a ton of fucking bricks. Stopping in the doorway, I saw Kon sitting on the couch watching something on television with Stormie. I hated to barge in on their father-daughter time, but I needed to get this shit off my chest before I was crazier than I already am.

His eyes connected with mine and he patted the empty spot on the couch on the other side of him. I shook my head and his brow lifted.

"I need to talk to you about something."

"Okay." He stood to his feet and excused himself, following closely behind me toward the living room. What I had to say, I couldn't say it in front of Stormie, not knowing how she was going to react. She liked me... at least for the moment. I wasn't sure if that like was going to quickly turn to hate once she found out that I was pregnant by her father and wasn't sure what I was going to do about her little sister or brother. "What's going on?" Kon quizzed me soon as we made it into the living room.

"I just got back from the doctor."

"What did they say?"

I gently sat down on the couch and stared down at my fiddling fingers. "I'm pregnant."

"Are you serious?"

He took the seat next to me and I felt his eyes burning a hole in the side of my head.

"I wish I wasn't."

"Why you say that?"

"I wasn't expecting a baby right now."

"But you're having one."

"You're not upset?" My eyes cut to him.

"Why would I be?"

"Because I'm pregnant."

"I wasn't expecting you to pop up pregnant, but since you are, I'm gon' take care of it."

"Just like that?"

"Just like that. So, when do you want to go get your stuff?"

"What do you mean?"

"You're pregnant, so you're moving in with me now."

"Don't you think it's a little too soon for that?"

"We're on our own timeline. If I want you to move in with me, then that's my fucking business. So, I'm gon' ask you again... when do you want to go and get your stuff?"

"Not right now. I just want to climb in bed and lay down for a little while."

"That's fine by me."

Rising to his feet, he scooped me up into his arms and carried me upstairs to his bedroom. Laying me down in bed, he took a step back and said, "If you need anything just let me know." And he left out of the room. I laid there just thinking about how much my life was about to change with this pregnancy.

Blessed

A couple of days later...

I woke up, turning over in bed, staring Sa'nai in the face. She was sleeping peacefully with her hair falling into her face. Brushing her hair back out of her face behind her ear, I kissed her gently on the center of her forehead. Her eyes opened and she gazed up at me.

"Good morning," she moaned, stretching.

"Morning." I pecked on her on the lips.

"How long have you been up?" she quizzed me.

"Not sure. I just been laying here watching you sleep and pass gas."

"You're a liar!" Her face flushed, and she quickly sat up in bed.

"No, I'm not. You've been farting for the longest. What the hell you ate last night?"

"Fuck you." She mushed me in the head and got up from the bed, treading into the bathroom.

"That shit can be arranged." I tossed the covers back and slung my legs over the edge of the bed. Before I could get up, my phone rang, and I quickly grabbed it. I thought maybe Kon was calling me, but Stephanie's name flashed across the screen. I hadn't heard anything from that motherfucker since we met at the restaurant. I actually thought she was bullshitting me, and I was going to have to hunt her ass down and deal with her.

"What?" I answered the phone.

"Someone must woke up on the wrong side of the bed." She laughed at her own joke, but I didn't find a damn thing funny. My eyes darted to Sa'nai standing in the doorway with her toothbrush shoved into her mouth. She'd been spending the night with me so much that I bought her a few things to keep in the bathroom.

"What the fuck do you want, Stephanie? I'm already two point five seconds away from hunting your ass down and putting you in an early grave."

"Calm down. I did exactly what you asked me to. I got the rest of the information on the shipment. The shit is going down today in like two hours."

"You wait until the day of to let me know some shit like that? I don't have enough time to come up with a fucking plan."

"Then I guess you're just going to have to wing it."

I wanted to reach through the fucking phone and wrap my got damn hands around her fucking throat.

"Text me the information and get the fuck off my phone." I hung up in her face before she pissed me off even more.

"Is everything okay?" Sa'nai asked me, nearing my side of the bed. She stopped in between my legs and I wrapped my arms around her waist, resting my face against her stomach.

"I have to go take care of some shit. You gon' be straight while I'm gone?"

"You always say that, but never tell me what you're about to do." She shoved me away from her and glared down into my eyes. "I know you don't live a normal life, Blessed, but I don't want to have to sit here and worry if you're going to walk back through that door or not."

"Baby girl, I've been doing this for a while now. You don't have anything to worry about." Standing to my feet, I went into the bathroom and started the shower.

"But I still feel like you're hiding something from me." She stopped in the doorway, resting her body against the frame.

Hooking her chin, I gazed deep into her eyes. "I'm not hiding anything from you. I don't tell you what's going on to protect you. It's for your own good. You want to get in the shower with me or what?"

"No, I'm good. I think I'm about to go check on Sapphire." She turned on her heels and exited the bathroom. I knew she was all in her feelings, that's why I went behind her, clasping her forearm.

"Don't tell me that you're mad with me."

I didn't have time for this bullshit right now. I had to hurry up and get ready and let Kon know what was going on. Those two hours were going to get here before I knew it and I'd been done lost out.

"No, I'm good. Go ahead." She grabbed some clothes out of the drawer and quickly tossed them on. She was ready to get the hell out of there with me.

"I don't have time for this shit right now. We'll talk about this later."

"No, we won't," she mumbled underneath her breath and I shook my head and went back into the bathroom.

I quickly took a shower and got dressed in all-black. As I headed out the front door, I called Kon to let him know that I heard from Stephanie and I was about to put the plan in motion. It wasn't a strong plan, just something I had come up with when I was in the shower.

Kon wasn't going to make it in time to the point and he didn't want me going alone, so he asked me to pick Don up and take him with me. I didn't mind because I didn't know exactly how many people were going to be inside the truck. Stephanie told me that it was supposed to be no more than two people, but I still needed to be prepared. We were going to hit the truck while it was en route and take the motherfucker back to our warehouse.

Pulling up to Don's trap, I blew the horn and waited for him to come to the car. He was still in his fucking feelings because we hadn't granted him permission to open the motherfucker back up. Kon and I were still trying to figure out how the fuck Thugga was able to find our shit in the first place.

Don jogged out to the car and hopped in alongside me. He rubbed his hands together with a smirk on his face.

"Let's get this show on the road," he said.

"Just don't fuck up and watch my fucking back."

Pulling away from the curb, I drove to the location Stephanie sent me on the phone. It was ducked off, but the truck was supposed to pass through there within the next fifteen minutes. I was nervous as fuck to see how the shit was going to fucking play out. Reaching into the back seat, I pulled my assault rifle from back there and cocked it.

"The truck should be here soon. When it's close, you park the car in the street where they can't go anywhere, and I'll hold the driver at gunpoint. You get the passenger and we make both of them step out of the truck, place a bullet in their ass and get the fuck out of here. You drive the truck and follow me to the warehouse. The plan is easy as fuck and should work long as you do what you're supposed to do."

"Bet." Pulling his gun from his waistline, he checked the clip and cocked it.

We sat there a few more minutes and I noticed the delivery truck cruising up the street.

"It's time." I quickly hopped from the driver's seat and Don climbed over into my seat. He pulled the car into the middle of the road and got out, hiding behind a garbage can.

The truck came to a halt and I quickly jumped out, aiming my gun at the nigga in the driver's seat. Don did the same with the other nigga. I swiftly yanked the door open to make sure he didn't try anything.

"Get out of the fucking truck."

The nigga had the fucking nerves to chuckle in my face.

"Do you know whose shit you're fucking with?"

"Fuck that nigga. I said get the fuck out of the truck."

He jumped down out of the truck, mugging me.

"Move that way." I nodded toward the right and he kept his hands up in the air to keep me from shooting his ass, but little did he know, he was going to fucking die anyway.

Pow!

I felt a burning sensation in my stomach. I clutched my stomach, feeling something wet oozing through my shirt.

"What the fuck?" Glancing down, I saw the blood and lifted my head. Don stood there with a smirk on his face and his gun aimed at me. "What the fuck are you doing?"

"I got a promotion," was all he said before firing at me again.

Pow!

Everything went black.

Sapphire

I stood off to the side, watching the groom as tears streaked down his face as his eyes locked onto his beautiful bride. That was one of the reasons why I loved the shit I did. To see the happiness on other people's faces when I accomplished whatever they wanted.

I would have still been stuck in the bed if it wasn't for Kon. He talked me out of the bed this morning to get here on time for this event I had been planning for the last few months. I was already paid in full and most of the shit was already put together. I could have easily had Sasha come and watch over everything. Kon thought it was best that I got out of the house and went back to work.

After the talk I had with him the night before, I felt a little bit better about being pregnant. At least I knew that he was going to be there for me, and I wouldn't be in this shit alone like most of the women I've come across.

The bride reached the groom and tears coated her face as well. She had one of the best MUA's in Miami, so even her tears didn't ruin her makeup. Watching them interact with each other, it had me wondering if I'd ever make it down the aisle to marry someone. Kon and I never talked about marriage, so I didn't know if that was something on the table or not. We were already moving a little bit too fast, I didn't want to ask him about that and scare him off.

Clapping hands brought me back to reality. I realized the

wedding was over with and I rushed out of the side door to go make sure the reception was ready for everyone's arrival. I did a quick run through to make sure that everything was in place.

"They're exiting the room now," Sasha spoke through the headset letting me know.

"Everything's in order," I told her and stepped to the side waiting for everyone to enter.

People began filing into the room. I watched how they admired the decorations that took me a while to fucking pull off. The DJ started the music and the bride and groom entered the room for the first time as Mr. and Mrs. Thomas. I stood there watching with misty eyes as they did their first dance.

My vibrating phone in my back pants pocket brought me from my thoughts. Pulling it out, I glanced down and saw Sa'nai was calling, so I stepped out of the room to see what she wanted.

"Can you believe that Blessed won't tell me what the fuck he does for a living? Like I'm about to have a baby with this man and feel like I don't know shit about him."

"Are you serious, right now?" Tilting my head back, I exhaled.

"I don't know shit about what Kon's ass does either. You can't force him to tell you something like that, Sa'nai."

"If I'm going to have a baby with this man, then I think I should know what the hell I'm getting myself into. He could bring anything to my fucking doorstep... put me or my baby in danger. At least if he told me what he did, then I could at least have a heads up or something."

"Sa'nai, I was in the middle of a reception. Can we just talk about this another time?"

"So, you agree with him?"

This had to be the fucking hormones that had her stressing about something like that.

"I'm not agreeing with anyone."

"That's not what it sounds like to me."

"Sa'nai, maybe you need to take you a nap or something. Don't push that man away over something stupid like that."

"So, I'm stupid now?"

I sighed, shaking my head.

"That's not what I fucking said."

"Whatever."

She ended the call and I slipped the phone back into my pocket. I'd just call and check on her once the reception was over and everything was cleaned up.

I eased back into the reception and the best man was giving a speech. I desperately wanted to sneak and have a drink to take my mind off things, but I knew I couldn't. That was going to be a downside to being pregnant.

I took a seat at the bar and snapped a few pictures of the reception to add to my business page. I made sure to take pictures of every event I did for sample photos.

The reception lasted a little longer than I thought it would. Eleven was rolling around and I had to watch over the people as they cleaned everything up and placed my decorations onto the truck. Most of the shit I bought, I could reuse at another event, then there were a few things that the bride sometimes wanted to take home as a reminder. Of course, I didn't mind.

Glancing down at my phone, I got a little bit more frustrated. I was ready to go home and eat a hot meal, shower, and climb in bed. I snuck a few pieces of chicken and stuff here and there to hold me over, but I didn't eat enough to fill me up.

"Can y'all move a little bit faster!"

"We're going as fast as we can, Sapphire," Sasha made known, carrying a box to the back door to load the truck.

I went back into the room where the wedding was held to make sure they got everything out of there. Once it was clear, I made my way toward the front door to make sure no trash was left in the parking lot. I always tried to make sure everything was clean whenever I left in case I needed to use that venue again for another event. It was always good to leave a good impression.

"Why must people be so fucking disgusting?" Bending down, I picked up a used condom with the end of my pen and tossed it into the trash can at the front door. Footsteps could be heard nearing me from behind. I swiftly turned on my heels and was faced with Chrissy. The mug on her face let me know she wasn't happy at all. "What the fuck are you doing here?"

I reached to grab my phone to call and let Kon know, but before I could get it, I felt a sharp pain in my abdomen.

"You thought you were going to have a baby with my man, bitch you're a fucking lie!"

She stabbed me again and I clutched my stomach, dropping to my knees.

"Checkmate bitch!" Her foot went straight across my face and everything went black.

To be continued...

CPSIA information can be obtained
at www.ICGtesting.com
Printed in the USA
LVHW092037061120
670968LV00007B/1092

9 798637 634835